RALEIGH REVIEW
LITERARY & ARTS MAGAZINE

VOL. 15.2
FALL 2025

RALEIGH REVIEW

VOL. 15.2 FALL 2025

PUBLISHER
Rob Greene

EDITOR-IN-CHIEF
Landon Houl

ACTING EDITOR-IN-CHIEF
Jessica Pitchford

FICTION EDITOR
Shel Senai

POETRY EDITORS
Chelsea Harlan, Samuel Piccone

ADVISORY POETRY EDITOR
D. Eric Parkison,
Leah Poole Osowski

EDITORIAL STAFF / FICTION
Dailihana Alfonseca, Alex Bryan,
Chas Carey, Abe Amy Chang
Madison Cyr, Robert McCready,
Kelly McCorkendale,
Jeff McLaughlin,
Allison Frase Reavis

BOARD OF DIRECTORS
Joseph Millar, Emeritus Chairman
Dorianne Laux, Emeritus Vice Chair
Landon Houle, Member
Bryce Emley, Member
Will Badger, Member
Tyree Daye, Member
Rob Greene, Member

ASSISTANT FICTION EDITORS
Erin Osborne

SENIOR COPYEDITOR
Elaina Ellis

COPYEDITOR
Kit Evans

EDITORIAL STAFF / POETRY
Alexander Gast, Erika Kielsgard,
Heather Lang-Cassera, Marty Saunders,
Melanie Tafejian

SOCIAL MEDIA COORDINATOR
Maggie Busch

ILLUSTRATOR
Nora Beers Kelly

LAYOUT & PAGE DESIGN
Alexis Olson

LITERARY PUBLISHING PROGRAM
Arianna Cuevas-Galarza

PUBLISHING ASSISTANT
William Chen

Raleigh Review, Vol. 15, No. 2, Fall 2025
Copyright © 2025 by *Raleigh Review*

Raleigh Review founded as *RIG Poetry*
February 21, 2010 | Robert Ian Greene

Cover collages by Geri DiGiorno
Cover design by Alexis Olson

ISBN: 978-1-59498-194-4

Raleigh Review is printed and bound via Fernwood Press in Oregon, U.S.A. and
distributed globally via Ingram.

Raleigh Review, PO Box 6725, Raleigh, NC 27628
Visit: raleighreview.org

RALEIGH REVIEW

table of contents

poetry cont. ————————————————————

nonfiction

book review.

illustrations

contributors

RALEIGH REVIEW

VOL. 15.2 FALL 2025

FROM THE EDITOR

I DON'T THINK I'VE EVER STARTED one of these notes by saying hello, but I find myself wanting to do that now in my Texan way. So hey, y'all! How are ya?

I feel like I need to pat you on the shoulder and get reacquainted because I've been away from the desk for a while, away from *Raleigh Review*. It's nice to be back. I'm happy to see you here.

I've been gone because I had a baby in January, and I've been spending as much time as possible with her. On the day I'm writing this note, summer is winding down, and my baby daughter has gone to daycare for the first time, an experience that was probably more traumatic for her parents than for her.

We're back home now, back in our stretch shorts and stained tshirts. We've eaten some Stage 1 pears (she has) and black bean burgers (we have) for a late lunch. We've played tambourine and cup stack and a homemade game we call Chicken Sweat. We've practiced being on our bellies and sitting up too. We've just finished reading a First Lift-a-Flap book called *Babies in the Ocean*, a sweet tale about two baby turtles who go out into the ocean to meet new baby friends including an octopus, a puffer fish, a whale shark, a dolphin, and—saving the best for last—a dugong.

I did have to look up that last one, so don't feel bad if you, too, have to do a quick Google search. In my defense, as I mentioned, I'm from Texas, central to be specific. I've only been to the ocean a handful of times. Dugong isn't a word I come across very often, but having a baby will teach you new things every day even if you're learning them from a board book.

My daughter loves *Babies in the Ocean*. Just showing it to her makes her eyes go big, her jaw drop. Her whole body rocks, and she immediately reaches, fingers excitedly, desperately clawing. You can practically feel the air around her go electric. This is the face, the body, the spirit of true wonder.

We'll leave *Babies in the Ocean* for a minute—don't worry, we'll come back to it—to talk about another great book I've come across recently, *Dear Writer: Pep Talks and Practical Advice for the Creative Life* by the poet Maggie Smith. Please check out this book if you haven't already. Smith has broken the book into chapters by what she sees as essential elements of the creative process. A whole chapter is dedicated to the idea of wonder. "There's no creativity without it," Smith says (27). She notes the ways in which her own kids and children in general come by imagery and metaphor "naturally [...] because they haven't been estranged from their imaginations and from their sense of newness in the world" (26).

That bright shininess can be cultivated even in something we do every day, another powerful idea Smith explores in a chapter called "Attention." "You don't need to be someplace new to see—or hear, or taste, or smell, or feel—something new" (19). Smith's experiences with her own children has helped me understand my daughter's excitement in new ways. It doesn't matter to her that we read *Babies in the Ocean* last night or five minutes ago. It doesn't matter that we walk down our driveway several times a day. It doesn't matter that she's heard me pop my lips about a thousand times. The adventure story, the fluttering leaf, the wonderfully startling smack—it's all new this time, this time, this time.

It's a good lesson or reminder, depending. Maybe as important as learning about dugongs.

I never had the pleasure of knowing Geri Digiorno. But hearing from those who did and considering her artwork, I believe she held on to that child-like sense of wonder. Digiorno's mixed media pieces share the same fresh perspective you'll find in this year's co-winners of the Geri Digiorno Multi-Genre Prize. In the winning entries by Ellen Kombiyil and Julie Marie Wade, you'll find the shock and beauty of unexpected juxtapositions, shapes, textures, images, words, sounds, and moments, and maybe you'll look up from the page and understand your world and someone else's a little differently. That's our hope, part of our mission here at Raleigh Review.

Maggie Smith argues that "wonder is a cousin of gratitude: to marvel at something," she writes, "is to deeply appreciate it" (25). In this issue, the second of our fifteenth year, you'll find writers and artists who, with their dazzling work, are praising, thanking, asking, feeling, wondering.

May you throw open this issue with a body atremble, with the same unbridled joy of a child with her first board book. Let it all be new and new again. ◆

We are grateful to you, readers.

Warmly,

Landon Houle, editor-in-chief

RAGE HEZEKIAH

MIDWINTER BEFORE SUNRISE

My teething son wakes
          at eleven, one, & four,
we dose him with Motrin,
          attempt to coax him

back to sleep. When I rise
          in the cold dark at five,
the cat grips a tattered
          mouse between his teeth—

blood trailing the kitchen floor.
          The tiny creature barely alive,
hides among our son's
          picture books, the cat

confuses play with torture.
          I wish I could damage
another to the edge. Before
          sleep I ask my wife how

many milligrams she's taking—
          is this familiar winter, or
how my son wails when
          I slice his banana too slowly?

Tearily tugs my sweatpants
        while I scramble his eggs.
Alex, still gone. Last night
        I dreamt I held him,

tousled his blond hair,
        lifted small sips of water
to his lips. I've never
        rescued anyone—
not even myself.

CHILDCARE

Sometimes I was high. I ate
your fancy cheese and drank
your whiskey. I pinched
your tiny son when he
wouldn't stop crying, then
sobbed in my cold car
after you came home. When
Bodhi puddled the seat
on the public bus, I pulled
the cord and we emerged
before our stop, rivers of piss
running down rutted grooves
in the floor. I got off
after the kids were asleep,
wore your slippers and napped
in your bed. Read an essay
about Dartmouth fraternities—
ordinary male torture. When
I'm not angry, I'm sad
for our men. My own
young son cutting
teeth and rolling over. I
text my father to tell him
I love him, thank him
for taking us to Friendly's
after the cat was hit by a car.
He wants to know
if it was our car. I thought
he'd remember piercing
a hole in the back edge
of our garden, digging
our pet's shallow grave.

AMANDA HODES

VIDEO GAME PROGRESS NARRATIVE

The choppy river,   lead-heavy,
               moves in reverse.
Escalator waves
               push against my chest
        in this Nintendo glitch:
I can't reach the next level   *can't reach*
            the past.

     At the edge of an invisible snowglobe,
  I march in place,
gliding slowly
             back to shore

   where I repeat this gesture
as long as it takes   to be saved.

  My brother, across the basement couch,
 hunts the remaining maps,
2D and rotating
        in a water-logged cave,
          glowing from the inside.

You have to dig around, he mumbles,
         find the pieces you need
    before you move on.

  But when we unlock the grassy platforms
    into the mountain,
        I cry.   Want to go back

with the fisherman who captions
            each bubble:
                Don't you love the weather today,
                    my dear?
Soft gibberish of his voice.

  A few years later, my brother will move out
and never return—

I sense this, perhaps, as he drags my avatar
            across the storyboard,
never technically
                        leaving me behind.

                The beveled graphics
                                melt darker
deeper   deeper into the mountain you go.

Here, he defeats the tentacled ghoul
                        with a lantern,
            leans into the cushion
                        controller on knee.

    In the cut scene, the mountain erupts
        into pixel.
A dynamite rockfall,   like Tetris,
            closes the entrance for good.

"*I can't reach the next level   can't reach*
the past."

— from *"Video Game Progress Narrative"* by Amanda Hodes

SOPHIA ZAKLIKOWSKI

PINCHER'S HOLE

MY HUSBAND was in Pincher's Hole, underwater, underground. When I rose at seven, he'd have been descending. As he sank, the sun which lifted over me would have thinned around him into sparse particles, spindly anchors of light plumbing the depth of him while in our kitchen I flipped the page of my Mommy To Be Calendar. It was the start of week thirty. The page said our baby was the size of a cabbage. Our baby was growing hair on its head and losing that other fine hair that covered its body in protective aura. I imagined if we all had fur.

My husband—my Myron—had left before dawn. I didn't notice when he got out of bed, but before he left for good he came back into the room and kissed my head. He kissed my bare belly, lifted like a slimy buoy in the leftover light of nighttime. He kissed it over and over, here and there, spinning a carousel around my belly and our baby inside. Then he ruffled my bush with the flat of his hand. "I love you and you."

"Don't forget your lamp. It's out back. I saw it there," I said.

"My lamp! How do you love me? Me and my head of scrambled eggs?"

"I want eight scrambled eggs for breakfast."

"I'll raise you ten," Myron said. "But you have to wait for me. Breakfast for dinner."

"I'm sleepy."

"Okay . . . shh ..." Myron lifted the blankie up to my chin. "I'll see you soon."

"Careful."

"I will."

"Bye-bye."

The next day the cops would give me a cup of cocoa to buffer their prodding: "'I'll see you later?' or 'I'll see you soon?'"

I'D BEEN TO PINCHER'S HOLE plenty of times. It was Myron's local dive spot. We used to drive around to lots of different dive spots, make whole trips of it—we'd been to Cauldron Sink in Texas and Knight's Sheath in Tennessee and elsewhere in Florida, Butter Bowl Reef and Christ's Cavern—but since I was pregnant, he stayed local.

Pincher's Hole is like a finger bored in cake. It is nearly perfectly round and small in circumference, not unlike a resort swimming pool. But downwards it goes on and on. You can tell just by the color. Linoleum-tile turquoise rims the shore, but within a few feet darkens to an impenetrable blue, packed as an ink stain. When a wind carries across the water, the ripples glint black.

There is a small wooden dock for divers to launch from. I would sun myself there, reading in my bikini, waiting for hours, nibbling on salami sticks, drinking a wine cooler or two, waiting for Myron to surface and look at me, sitting up, tan and sweating with the strings of my bikini scribbled across me. Even though he'd just seen the sublime, he'd pull his goggles down and look at me like I was alchemizing.

"Come 'ere, my river rat." Face glistening with snot, pink and trimmed in purple depressions from the suction. How I'd slink to him . . .

Sometimes I snorkeled in the pool, saw how the limestone plummeted through color and into benthic black, felt the haptic compression of the sheer walls around me like cymbals about to clang together. But I never experienced what Myron did. Down in the caves, he said, was like being inside of a great unknown creature—triped corridors, capillary squeezes, walls the texture of tumors. Trying to figure out the life of the thing from the inside-out.

I asked him why it was called Pincher's Hole, if it was after a Mr. Pincher or if pincher referred to the tightness of the crannies or what, but Myron didn't know and wasn't interested in those kinds of mysteries. And then I couldn't bring myself to look it up, once the caves were associated with such greater mystery, the location of his poor body. I thought on that enough.

Myron was interested in bigger mysteries, though I'm not sure he'd be comfortable with my naming them "mysteries." He was interested in outer space, the innumerable rainforest species, Prehistoric man, caves. The day after he went missing, the news began covering a volcanic eruption in Iceland. I kept up with it, for him. I watched clips online, noting how the black and yellow speckled lava flows looked like city sprawl at night.

I went to the site every day to watch over the procession of divers. Cameramen irised around me, cordoned off by a freckling of cops. I was the pupil, watching, centered.

First they sent the scuba cop down to retrieve Myron's body, but the scuba cop couldn't find him. In the next few days, a dozen different expert divers went into the caves to look for his body and couldn't find a trace of him. They went as far into the system as they could; two of them almost died themselves looking for him, narrowing into sticky crevices beyond what they should've. People die all the time in caves, but people don't go missing in them. Unless Myron had forced himself into an impossible space, his body should've been findable. That's what the cops said. That he'd knowingly squirmed past the point of return. That he drowned himself.

I couldn't logic my way out of it and didn't try to. Caves are places beyond logic, and you can't explain that to someone who doesn't get it. People saw a pregnant lady and some stuck husband who saw his only way out: to get more stuck. I can see it the way they saw it too. I'm not stupid. I just know. Our baby kicked and kicked then, more than ever.

WHEN MYRON DISAPPEARED, the first person I called was my mom's boy-friend. We spoke on day one, but I have absolutely no memory of it. I just raved.

After that first week I called again. "Hi, Stuart." My voice echoed in the phone, shameful baby-talk, like I was calling for money. Hearing my voice like that was like finding a stranger's things stranded in a culvert—bundles of twigs, shells, underpants—evidence of an unsettled life to make you walk faster.

I lay on the couch, twitchy, undone, so thirsty I could see tinsel falling from the ceiling. I updated him on the situation.

"Anyways," I said. "How are you? How's Colorado?"

"Oh please, forget me, forget Colorado." Stuart was from Tallahassee but moved to Colorado, Myron's homestate, at his suggestion after my mom died. He lived in a ranch-themed retirement community that touted multiple backup generators in case of snowstorms—the elderly population are disproportionately killed by cold exposure. Things that once to me seemed kind now seemed cruel—the idea of Christmas, considerations for the aged. . . Stuart met my mom in a seniors' tango class at the rec center. I liked him very, very much. They dated for four years until my mom's diagnosis and then continued on through until her death. I wish they'd met ages ago, even if it meant I was never born. Stuart was Black and if it was just me and him out together, nobody ever assumed that our relationship was kin.

"Doesn't that bother you?" I asked him once.

"Things are never how they look," he said. "I'm used to that." Before he retired, Stuart was an autopsy photographer. Leg bones up through a jumper's shoulder bones, faces wiped to static thrown from the beds of pickups. He liked to wax poetic about the lives behind the messes—I think that's what he was getting at with his response, but it may have just been a redundant question to ask a seventy-three-year-old Black man, 'doesn't that bother you.' I wanted to raise our baby to be good and thoughtful and worried they'd only be half as good and half as thoughtful without Myron there too.

"Well, it's snowing, but it's not sticking," Stuart said. There was a beat and we listened to the hollow hum of the space between our telephones. "You sure you don't want me to fly out there? Could feel good to have some family with you. I'm family. "

I didn't recall having already discussed this in our blacked-out call. I actually wanted that very badly.

"No, no," I said, sticking to my supposed guns. "It's just that I need to get something straight. I always trusted Myron not to die. He said so. He promised that he would never get into trouble down there and I trusted him completely. But you know what everyone's saying. They're saying suicide—and that's impossible, plain idiotic. So: either he drowned on purpose, which he didn't, or it was an accident and I have to stop trusting him. Without him even around to defend himself. How unfair is that? I feel ashamed, like a bad wife."

"Don't talk like that. I think the only one you're not being fair to is—YOURSELF."

I'd been so keen on talking this through with Stuart and feeling some comfort, but now he was saying exactly what I knew he would say, I might as well have had this conversation with myself. I needed objectivity. He loved me too much.

"Thanks," I said. "I feel better. I'm gonna go clean up. Talk soon."

I hung up. I stood with my phone like a graham cracker in my hand, feeling inert. Afraid to start thinking, to converse with myself, I made another call. I called Myron's cave buddy Dino and asked him to come over. Dino was a big guy, not like my Myron. Myron was sinewy. You could see the shreds of his tendons move around in his arms and his belly button was pulled taut surrounded by little bricks of muscles. Myron had an Adam's apple that bobbed about in his throat, curls which loped down his head like mountain goats, and a big nose he'd press into my pussy. I could get lost describing Myron. What I mean is that Myron was skinny and Dino was big, which can make cave diving difficult. He often couldn't go as far into systems as Myron could. Myron would explain in exacting detail what was beyond the points Dino could access, and Dino—an architect—would draw up these incredible maps. I asked Dino to bring his map of Pincher's Hole.

"Hi sweetheart," he said at the front door. He gave me a long hug. Since Myron disappeared, I'd only been hugged by the phony cop psychologist, who was me-shaped; when we hugged our shoulder bones knocked together. Dino hugging me felt like I was being swallowed up out of myself.

We finally pulled apart and I said, "I'm okay."

I'd cooked some frozen Indian food dinners, four of them because I didn't want him to be hungry, and I knew I could eat two myself with our baby, which was now the size of a coconut. We sat at the round kitchen table eating everything all mixed up together and not talking. Dino looked like a wrestler, was big and blonde with a shoebox jawline. He stuffed himself into button-up shirts and khakis for his architect job; he looked like a wrestler on trial.

I sucked the curry off the peas and collected them in a pocket of my mouth, eyeing him. One by one I popped the peas between my teeth. This was what I liked to do. Myron knew about this. I was lonely and part of me wanted to explain this quirk to Dino, but how could I? How could I do that to Myron? I'd have rather cheated on him and slept with Dino than do that. And I thought about it too. I was so lonely and horny, and I knew 100% that Myron was dead—that wasn't the mystery—so it wasn't really cheating, was it. I popped the peas in my mouth and looked at Dino with oily slivered eyes.

"Darling," he said, "I don't have the map. I don't think that's a good idea."

"I asked you to bring it." I dribbled the peas onto a sheet of newspaper I'd ripped out about the volcano in Iceland. They suddenly tasted vile. In the newspaper photo were a bunch of sheep, black and white lava phlegming up into the sky in the distance. "Sorry," I said.

"I know you did, baby. But I really don't see how that would help right now."

"Not you too."

"What?"

"Deciding what I think. You didn't even bring it with you? It's not in the car?"

"No," he said.

I put my feet up on a chair. "You're being so patronizing." Myron hated when I was being patronizing. This is something we'd argue about. Now I understood.

"It seems to me—I don't know for sure, I'm not saying what you think—but it seems to me that you aren't fully grasping the gravity of what has happened."

"Myron died and I am going to have his baby," I said.

"No," he said. "The gravity."

I asked Dino to leave.

Back when Myron was alive, each week I would make a dish inspired by the fruit or vegetable from the Mommy To Be Calendar. The day Myron disappeared, I'd gone to the grocery store and bought a red cabbage to make borscht with for dinner, even though he'd said all that about ten scrambled eggs. As I was cutting it up, I noticed how the leaves looked like liver, deep burgundy purple and rubbery. The following week I made a coconut cake and after Dino drove off I took it to bed and ate directly from it with a fork. When I was full I put it on the bedside table and went to sleep. Every few hours I'd wake, itchy all over—a new pregnancy symptom—and take some blind bites.

THE NEXT DAY Myron's mother, Bea, arrived at Pincher's Hole. I already knew that she was in town. She'd flown out from Colorado after his disappearance and was staying at a hotel nearby, too shaken to come stand on the grass.

I really didn't want to see her. I'd only met her twice, but I knew of the two of us I was going to be the one expected to attend to the other.

Bea brought along her neighbor from the hotel, a woman with a darkly tanned face loose as a pair of stockings. She wore black leggings. One of her calves was severely swollen.

"Where do you feel him?" Bea asked the woman. She said this again and again, a pot put on to boil and then forgotten—sputtering, burning. Her eyes looked horrible, wet but dry like spit out sucked on candies. She clung to me, our arms linked, her nails dug in.

The woman then limped in quiet loops around the hole, her leg like a violin case, her eyes shut and quivering. As she walked, Bea grabbed at my arm like she was trying to climb up. "Bea, please."

"Isn't she incredible? She is a conduit to subterranean pulses, she says it pains her very much, so I cannot imagine a more perfect match. She found me, at the continental breakfast waffle station, said she could sense my suffering. She called my grief palpable, my aura the color of iron ore. I spilled the pitcher of batter all over the carpet. So attuned. In the days since I met her, she has relieved my aura down to purple. Aubergine."

The medium had taken off her shoes and was marching in spot with little padding steps. "I can tell she's on to something," Bea whispered.

When the medium approached us she kept her eyes shut. Her eyeliner had been tattooed on.

"He is profoundly present," she said. "Pro-found-ly."

"Oh God!" Bea cried, falling through my linked arm. Myron and I were at the beach once at the same time as a bunch of backhoes dumping sand. They do this in Florida to try and replenish the beaches with beach from elsewhere. Myron told me about 'sand mafias' in India, Hungary, Mexico, Greece, Jamaica, Singapore, all over. Rival sand gangs steal sand back and forth. Beaches disappear overnight, people are killed. "The world is running out of the very things that make it a world," he said. I found this funny and sad and perfectly evocative of him and how he saw things. We went swimming—suspended with the tractors behind us and oil rigs out beyond us—and I felt how rough and ready life is, how pure that makes it, like a play put on by children. I thought of this as she fell, a heap of earth collapsing into me. I picked her back up.

"We know he's here," I said. "Maybe you should go talk to one of the divers." I handed Bea over to her neighbor.

"May I?" the medium asked. Her eyes were open now. I think that she was wearing orange contact lenses. She held her hands open before my stomach. I nodded and she pressed her hands onto me. Slowly she began to rub at the base of my womb. I felt the trace of her rings like snail slime under my blouse.

"It's the size of a coconut," I said.

"She is connected to her father. In a way that could prove to be more enlightening than any of this—them, me. But are you connected to her? Can you hear what she's telling you? How can you respond if you aren't listening?"

I screwed her hands off of me and cussed the two of them out. Bea was weepy and trying to swat the words away from her. The medium just gazed at me in a way I found particularly condescending. All of this condescension! I felt like I could cry but was very bored of crying. It didn't help anymore, it only made me feel dehydrated and dumb. I waddled off to the dock and laid down on my back. Splayed out supine on the wood, my womb started to contract. I'd read about practice contractions in the

Mommy To Be Calendar. I watched the sky, squeezed and squeezed like a wrung sponge, practicing on my little stage for the real thing.

Later in the afternoon a diver came up with something he'd found. There was hubbub. News crews funneled onto the banks and craned their cameras out over the blue, water lapping up over their dedicated feet. The diver had found a mask wedged with manipulation into a deep crack. I was brought over to identify it. Bea wailed in the medium's lank arms. It took one second for me to know it wasn't his.

"Are you sure?" the police asked.

"Of course I'm sure!"

"My poor broken boy!" Bea cried.

"Let's sleep on it."

"Depression! Did I give him depression?" Bea was holding the head of the medium in her hands like a Magic 8 Ball, shaking for an answer other than maybe.

"I Sharpied a heart on the inside of every one of his masks. You could tilt the black rubber and the black marker would catch the light and glow red. I did this to all of them. See? Nothing."

"Maybe you missed one. Thought that counts," the cop said.

"What, I forgot to love him like that one time? Plum forgot?"

Myron hadn't liked cops one bit, and his mother was his mother. I went home early.

I tried calling Dino to ask about the map again, but it kept going to voicemail. Then I made an entire baking sheet of bacon in the oven and crumbled it over stovetop popcorn. Against my will I tried to get in touch with the baby inside of me, but instead started thinking of my own mother.

When she was diagnosed, I moved back in with her. It was at the start of Myron and me. She had her colon removed and for a year I cared for her. I emptied her colostomy bag, cooked for her, stroked her hair to get her to sleep when she was overwhelmed by fear of death. Myron would visit us. He wrote these silly jokey songs and performed them for us on his guitar—a song about the longest English word, a song about needing to take a poop at Nascar. He brought my mom rocks from his cave-diving that he left out in his yard during the full moon to energize. This is what I thought of while I ate my greasy popcorn.

I couldn't sleep that night. At 3 AM I took a bath. Lights out and co-cooned in warm water, I imagined I was my own child deep in the dark of my womb. Stay there, I told her, get stuck too. I woke at dawn, my ear all full of water.

AFTER THE GOGGLE DEBACLE, I stopped going to Pincher's Hole. It was a charade. All I wanted was to go into the caves myself, to get a sense of the other world he understood. I watched countless crappy videos of the systems people had made on their dives, but no one went as deep as Myron did, I knew that.

I'd go into the garage and put Myron's gear on. With his mouthpiece in my mouth, I'd masturbate. Clamped and drooling on the rubber, I washboarded my passive bits.

My baby grew to the size of a jicama, then a pineapple, cantaloupe, and honeydew. The doctor rubbed jelly over it and talked to me about the three Cs of grief—choose, connect, communicate. She wiped the jelly off with a tissue and told me about the impact of stress on a fetus. Neighbors continued to feed me, but less of them, so that the meals became redundant. I felt ginormous. I slept like a spoke in bed. My face was always ruddy. Before the mirror I scraped my fingers over my cheeks and thought of the lava fields, all that which is deep within becoming molten and violently singular, then rising, showing through.

Dino offered to pay for therapy. I said okay, and asked him to come over to work out the details. On the couch, I nestled my head into his Great Plains chest. He cooed over me and I let it all out for him. Sniffling back together, I started rubbing his big belly. I looked up at him, my eyes bowls of milk, and kissed him. He fucked me in slow, long strokes, like the cadence of grasshopper song. It really did feel good. "Please," I said, the breath nearly out of me. In some slurry of dirty talk I begged him for what I wanted: for him to cum for me and for him to bring me the map that showed everywhere Myron had been in Pincher's Hole.

He pulled himself out of me so quickly. "Oh God, brother," he spit. "Forgive me, brother."

Trust felt to me as ancient and misinterpreted as childhood.

"It's okay, Dino."

"He drowned himself. I think you need to, need to, accept that. Appreciate that. You are not doing well."

Here he was, back at it, telling me about myself. I picked up a hefty bottle of lotion from the bedside and smacked him on the head, to prove him right and wrong at the same time, to show him I was complicated and beyond his stupid adages.

He left, forgetting his leather belt which I threw away after letting the garbage disposal eat at the tongue end for a bit.

Week thirty-seven, my baby was the size of a leaf of chard and the search ended. Nothing conclusive had been found, nothing but the goggles that weren't his wedged with supposedly decided force into the webbed limestone. On this alone the case was put to rest as a suicide.

"A body doesn't disappear unless somebody wants it to," a cop had said to me a month back.

"You have no idea about these caves," I said. "Not a single clue."

After they'd cleared out, that first emptied night, I returned to Pincher's Hole. Bugs played whining fiddles in the surrounding amphitheater of jungle. A half-full moon reflected in skittering silver bracelets across the pool. The small orange lamp that hung from the edge of the diver's dock lit the water below in a kettle of algae green. It was still and quiet, yet I couldn't fully shake the trace of them, all the others and their equipment, their probing. Under my feet I could feel how the earth was changed, tilled by them. I could smell swamp, fecund and rainwarm, but also something different; the air smelled ambiguous.

I bent for a stone and threw it in the water. It made a great thump like smacking someone's belly when they aren't expecting it. The moon and the dark marbled and tore together towards me. I found a bigger rock and threw it. Then another, this one dense and large as a man's head—I had to go underhand. Edging in my espadrilles at the tree line, I found another, bigger yet. I kept at this, hunting for heavier and heavier rocks. The last one I went for I had to put my whole body into. I couldn't straighten my legs. Huffing, I inched forward with the whole of it enwrapped, my torso, my breasts, my womb—my pleading womb, my pelvis and thighs all touching it, my chin locked over its crown. At the hole, I forced myself into the rock, to send it from me. It fell a foot or so before me at the waterline of the bank and rolled, just barely. Waves lapped at it, this new island rising from the mud. I tried to catch my breath but couldn't. As the pantings of exertion passed, I continued to labor over my breaths, overcome by another kind of effort, a rescission of effort.

STUART ATTENDED THE BIRTH. He brought a cowhide to swaddle her in and a collection of poetry about motherhood. My baby came and I pushed her out. My canal clung to her yet out she came. I saw her and thought how she was nothing like a fruit or vegetable. She was inventing herself. When I suckled her, her lips moved like caterpillars. It felt like a rubber band snapping at me, calling me to attention.

I brought her home and set up Stuart in the living room.

Just after I gave birth, Stuart had taken a polaroid of my baby and me together in the hospital bed, still covered in each other and amnesiac. It was the same camera he'd used for all his years of recording corpses. The picture slithered out of the camera's vent and together we watched the image swell. On film the scene appeared washed in green, the moment brined and pickled. My gaze stuttered—it couldn't land anywhere. The pixels spliced and I saw myself and her in my arms and everything around us as inseparable, a chimera.

Tucked in on the couch, Stuart admired the photo.

"Lights out?" I asked.

He took off his glasses, laid the photo down. He nodded and smiled at me with his familiar, plain compassion but it seemed entirely new, and I felt the gonging remembrance that love is reinvented every second and wished I'd asked him to come to me long before. I flipped the switch. In the dark I could hear him making hearty swallows. "You're strong," he said.

In my bedroom, I looked hard at my baby, and I saw Myron. Blurry, as if looking at him underwater with my eyes raw open. Like I could just blow on her face, clear off the me-ness of her and the her-ness of her, and he'd be there beneath.

Sometimes when I used to have trouble sleeping, Myron would illustrate a cave for me. I'd close my eyes and he would lead me through.

You're descending, you can descend quickly but must remember that however far you descend you must rise up from, and the ascent is much slower. At the first shelf, go left. It narrows. Go head first. Don't kick at all. Silt will blind you otherwise. Use your hands. Good, you're in. There are five inches above you and five below you, like you're in the gut of a snake. The space grows tighter and tighter. Now turn out your light. Doesn't it feel warm to be held this close?

I'm descending, I can descend quickly but must remember that however far I descend I must rise up from, and the ascent is much slower. At the first shelf, I go left. It narrows. I go head first. I don't kick at all. Silt will blind me otherwise. I use my hands. I'm in. There are five inches about me and five below me, like I'm in the gut of a snake. The space grows tighter and tighter. Now I turn out my light. It feels warm to be held this close.◆

SARA FEMENELLA

A BRIEF HISTORY OF TOUCH

At first it was a game.
Touch. Not touch.

It was what I wanted,
it was not what I wanted.

I knew all the warnings.
There was a hole

in my warnings
where his hands got in.

After the game it became
a performance.

*See, here is the daughter
I can be with the lights off.*

I use my hands, my mouth.
I use my warnings exactly how he likes it.

*See, I am the kind of woman
he likes best.*

In each of my warnings a woman
shows another woman how to behave.

*See, I am that kind of woman
all the way down.*

That's how women learn
their history, from the holes

in what we were warned.
Every time a man

says *tell me you want it,*
every time a man touches

the shimmer
of my performance,

I pull a new trick
from inside me

like a trembling rabbit
from a black satin hat.

MAG GABBERT

[IT'S TRUE: ONCE YOU'VE GROWN]

It's true: once you've grown up, the very idea of a bouquet can be thrilling. Today at the boutique, my younger cousin is trying on a dress while Louis Armstrong's "Moon River" plays overhead. In the not-so-distant past, Apollo 13 circles its target but never lands. My cousin twirls, shows us a long, close row of pearl buttons down the back. Beyond glass doors, shredded silk from a spiderweb drifts by on the wind and I'm watching it—I remember a building at the heart of my city with a giant, lit orb atop a high, thin tower. There was a time when you could sit inside the sphere, eat chilled shellfish with little forks, and slowly spin. Crescent shrimp, nebulous oysters. And so a thought, much like a wedding, occurs: how to describe the loneliness of Copernicus? Was it like turning himself away while everyone else watched the sunset?

[NIGHTS LIKE THIS ARE WHEN]

Nights like this are when I want to text my ex. Ask, what have I missed? Let enough snow fall on a flat roof and you might see it: there's a point at which too much weight will become a drain. When *avoid* will break, become *a void*. I guess this is called gravity, or gravitas—that feeling of being drawn in. Here at the bar, they have a boxing match on every TV. First it looks like a dance, with two men circling the ring. Then their bodies cave, veer toward a hugging tournament. There have been times when I feared one outcome so much, I caused it. Couldn't resist, like Orpheus. Times when I ended good relationships. D'Arcy Thompson wrote, "The form of an object is a diagram of forces." Which brings us to diamonds, and the pressure surrounding them. It's enough to buckle me.

"First it looks like a dance, with two men circling the ring."

— from *"[Nights like this are when]"* by Mag Gabbert

AMBER FLAME
AT THE RISK OF SELF

HER LOVER WANTED A HOME. I will grow her a whole world, she said to herself, and busied herself seeding and weeding, pruning and anxiously awaiting fruit. She took a pickaxe to the red earth, hauled bags of topsoil. Her lover was thirsty, and so she took up a shovel. Dug deep into the desert bedrock in search of water. When they fucked, her lover left her voiceless, wrung of moisture on wet sheets.

She suspected her lover had skipped town when her mouth dried, suddenly and irrevocably, midway through the washing. By the time she had beat out the blood and cum stains and pinned the last of the linens on the line, her belly protruded, a tight drum sloshing water. Her tongue, swollen to fill her mouth, a small furred still thing.

Next to dry were her hands. But her hands always roughened on washing day; surely some oil would help. Her palms seemed to drink the moisture to no effect, while her cuticles peeled and shredded before her eyes. The door to the house shuffled over the bump in the clay floor as if this were any other day.

When she knew for certain her lover had left town, she lay down to weep her tears for a little while. This is what she said to herself: I will weep for a little while. And so she commenced, her head heavy on her hands, themselves a cushion from the packed earth despite their red and splitting nail beds. The tears fell to the hungry mouth of the floor. In not too long a time, the woman rose, feeling empty. She marked how the clay was not muddy or even damp; the thin skin of her foot snagged the curling ceramic edge of its cracked plating, slicing open cleanly as broken pottery is wont to do. There was no blood.

When next she was able to rise, so had the moon, full and orange and reminding her of harvest. The woman felt thirst clog her throat, the soft insides of her cheeks sticking tacky to her molars. She rose up from the barren crater she was making of her home. This is what she said to herself, I will rise up from this barren crater. This is my home. Outside, the desert had delighted in a slow feast of the water-heavy plums and melons her lover desired, saplings succumbing and withered in the heat. After the well drew nothing and the bucket thumped hollow, the rope slipped from her hands and she grew still. From her garden beds, growing wild peppers and trees dripping sweet citrus fruit waited with her, patient and listening for rain. ◆

RACHEL ROTHENBERG

HALF SISTER AS HARBOR SEAL AMONGST THE SHARKS

Surfers tell me sharks won't sleep.

They must be wakeless

cut lidded, sharks have no veiled desire to undream, eyes

arrowed to the seal that whiskers potbellied between the lit

chop above and their empty darted hunger.

Surfers won't trawl the depths for shark teeth whet to screws

what stratum grinds

their hissing spiracles to surface.

I watch them notch a count of seals, surface map drawn to align

the sea's dormant carnivores: here, a plush overwintered torso

there, its eddying exhalation.

Doomed fuselage

of back and belly, palmed and armless as a plane fallen to the sea

wing-clipped, unruptured: one disaster averted

another imminent.

Surfers know what doesn't break us

will drown us instead, that the sea's foam lattice is trapdoor

and not netting, riptide and not buoy.

I imagine my grasp

       knuckled under her skin, the seal's mammalian skeleton

hindlimbs split to hip beneath the flippers.

          Her long rakey toes fanned out, claws

that might have shredded the line-up

                      gouged their neoprene calves

      shimmied the bark to safety in some other landlocked evolution.

The surfers' knees knock dry in their wetsuits.

      The seal's legs stubbed and bound, cinched in their flexed fin.

I tell them

      no body's implicit metaphor will redraw our hem and halt.

The surfers would have me brave it alone

      chinned to their white boards, saltbleached and slatted

         pickets staked between all their unventured rescues

and my life here sink-lined

          my spears for salvage.

HOPE KELHAM

WATER DAMAGE / EARTH ROT ELEGY

for Madayln

"Show me / Eternity, and / I will show / you Memory"
  —Emily Dickinson

"You have gone (which I lament), you are here (since I am addressing you)"
  —Roland Barthes

We loiter the woods lining   the trailer park entrance
        You flee   in a haunt with me

There, we make a cot of intimates   left in laundromat dryers
          Your depression festers   with the consequence of survival

Juniper skies do flock   swallowing the waft of the dozen
murder   who swamp the cul de sac

We cough black feathers   as you coo into my shoulder

I sing the siren   palm the shell of   every cicada,
          turning it over   like a stone   or the
almost

memory of jumping naked   into the stream,
                    the swimming hole   swollen with algae
        We watch the light eddy   hold our breath in belows

You told me love   was running   beside us
          Your legs longer   than lungs

The swimming hole bloomed
         under the weight of us
     love living long enough   to reveal the dearth of a paradise
lost to a relapse   white capsule of your palm
       The swimming hole bloomed   storm green

There,
     I undressed indelicately,   slept in heat   under the want of us,
the evergreen sex of us,   superimposing my two tangled lips
     on the tops of your eyelids   to pin your dreams
In them,
     we might watch light move   through a chain-link fence, perch

in plastic   lawn chairs   as the estuaries
     empty like half-filled theaters

I burn agony blue and
there,
     you always   live on my tongue, commanding my kisses   as wet
as the payphone   in the city isthmus fires

Without you, plumes have become   the stuff of throats
The time capsule   left dilapidated, floods

the diorama of us,   the wallpaper,   sogs, streaks
     with mud, your hemline   melts in my mouth

Your hemline
     dollies, collects the weight
       of the men who only ever   wished to see our bodies
a foraged thing,

       You search my lips,
    you scorch them,
      Fold my body
    into the howling draft of yours, white lace on white lily—

a grief that insists—
your violet low lows, I excavate,

    find your voice
             still carrying across the water

KRISTINE NOWAK

FOR THE PARROT IN THE PARROT SHOP

This woman is telling me how she loves
parrots, her finger stroking the forehead
of a bird wrapping itself through the cage
in every way it can: the hooks of long
black toes curled around one bar, another
bar angled in its splintering beak.
                              She tells me
she is mesmerized by their beauty, those jet
eyes set gleaming in their pearl sockets,
the prisms of scarlet feathers tending
towards sunlight, sapphire.
                         The curve
of this bird's wings and neck are bare
and mangled skin, the pale roots
of the feathers visible; the bird
keeps tearing itself down towards
the bones.
          She has an African Gray, too,
but Scarlet Macaws have always
been her favorite.
                   The bird's body is a shadow
of something far from here.
                              This woman
says love, love,
love.

EMMA DEPANISE

INVENTORY OF FAILED TRANSFORMATIONS

Dough that just won't rise, a plum
    refusing to ripen. The fruit

        not in the frosted
    glass bowl today, corroded

batteries in the keyboard. Film
    of another family left

        in a pawned video
    camera. Their undeveloped

        smiles. Poppies in the field
    unfacing the sun. The washing

machine as it confuses
    my clothes, tries to tumble

        tags into sea glass.
    Sea glass. The few coins

    I hold. Bread in the yard,
uneaten by the birds.

M.J. STEINBACH
RESCUED LATE

MY PARENTS lived under the same roof but were by no means loving or even friendly with each other. Their relationship was closer to that of estranged roommates. I have one older sister who is just about the opposite to me in every respect. She was, and still is, very bookish, studious, rigid, uptight, snobbish—and these qualities made her my parents' favorite, for some reason. Sure, I actually helped on the farm, growing the crop that kept the family alive, while she spent the majority of her time in her bedroom reading and writing—things my parents never did but highly respected. I did fine in school, but I wasn't an intellectual, and I valued goofing off more than getting good grades. And I didn't learn the lesson to just shut up and take orders until the Academy, so I was constantly mouthing off to my parents whenever there was a chore I didn't want to do. My father didn't take back-talk. In fact, back-talk invited the back of his hand. He was often unpleasant, but over the years, I've come to understand—maybe even sympathize with—some of the unpleasantness. Being poor, working all day long under the hot sun, then coming home to do more work, in a house where your family feels like strangers, where your wife is just as miserable as you are, your daughter looks down on you with contempt, and your son eats up just about half your earnings in food and refuses to do a single thing he's told without giving some lip. Listen, poor rural life can be miserable, and I get why the neighbor's wife was found hanging in their barn.

Her husband found her like that, neck strained and bruised, face frozen in a grimace, body dangling from a beam, stool kicked over below her feet, and a cow fussing in the corner. Upon discovery, he ran directly to our house. We really didn't know him all too well, other than that he was also poor, barely scraping by. He was out of breath, so we could barely understand what he was saying, but he finally got it out: his wife was dead. She'd hanged herself, he'd said, running a hand up an imaginary noose trailing from his neck up, up, up. I felt a spasm round my own neck, rubbed at it but then dropped my hand to my side like a weight, shoved it in my pocket, embarrassed when I noticed the man's eyes fixed on me.

I'm not saying it was right, what she did. Because it wasn't. But I understand her wanting to leave. My father called an ambulance for the man and his dead wife and told me to go to the barn to meet the paramedics when they arrived. I argued with him, told him I didn't want to. Why couldn't my sister do it? She was older, after all. Well, that remark warranted a slap across my face. He pushed me out the door and locked it behind me.

I wiped the blood from my nose with the back of my hand, swore at my old man a bit under my breath, and then left, resigned to my assignment. I took the long way, dragging my feet through the gravel path, walking slowly to the neighbor's. It would take a while for the ambulance to get all the way out here anyway, and I didn't want to spend any more time there than I needed to. That walk is stamped in my memory, seeing the red barn in the distance, surrounded by seemingly endless fields of corn shouldering the weight of the heavy blue sky. It was an insult—how nice a day it was, given it all.

Before I even made it to the barn, still a ways up the gravel driveway leading to it, I saw two dogs laying by the open door. As soon as they spotted me, they ran to greet me, barking and yapping, frenzied. They ran round me in circles, to the barn, back to me, and to the barn again, trying to convey a sense of urgency. How could I tell them it was too late? That there was no need to rush? I finally got to the barn and, keeping my eyes on the ground, I pulled the big double doors closed without looking in. The dogs barked and barked and barked, jumping up and scratching at the door.

"Shhh. There's nothing we can do now."

I sat on the ground, leaned back against the barn door, and tried to calm the two dogs. They sat on either side of me, whining as I stroked their heads, whimpering until we saw the ambulance approaching in the distance. They left my side to greet the paramedics—to urge them to hurry, rush, help—leading them to the barn as they did me a half hour earlier. Two men stepped out and ambled over.

"She's in there," I said, jutting my chin over my shoulder. One of the dogs was scratching at the door.

"Is it bad?"

I shrugged. One of them opened the big doors. The dogs rushed in past him, almost knocking him over.

"Geez," one of them said.

"Yeah," said the other.

I stood up and started walking back up the path, away. To anywhere else.

"Hey!"

I looked back. One of them was standing in the doorway.

"We need your help, kid."

I didn't argue, I knew it was coming. This wasn't a time for lip—and besides, he wasn't my dad. I walked back and forced my gaze up from the ground. The woman was wearing her Sunday best, probably the nicest dress she owned. Her eyes were open, fixed on a spot in the distance. I wondered what the last thing she saw was, what she was seeing now. The dogs were licking her bare feet and ankles. One of the paramedics tried to shoo them away to keep her body from swaying from the noose. The cow in the corner was silent, eating hay.

I picked up the turned over stool below her naked, dirty feet and set it near the cow to get it out of the way. And I gave a glance around for her shoes, by the way, but found none. The men patted their pockets, rummaged in their bag a bit before asking if I had anything sharp to cut the rope. I told them I did and held out my pocketknife with a shaky hand. But, they didn't take it. Instead, they motioned me over, closer to the body, further implicating me in the ordeal. I held the knife out again, thrusting it to one of the men. But he shook his head.

He bent, wrapping his arms around my legs, lifted me to be face-level with the woman, her mouth agape, eyes dilated and fixed. I held my breath and sawed at the rope as fast as I could. The other man wrapped his arms around the woman's thighs to catch her when she was freed, his face buried in the front of her dress.

All the while, the dogs were whining and barking, jumping up and pawing at the woman's legs, scratching at the men. They tried to kick and swat them away, but to no avail. The last bit of rope finally frayed, snapped, and her body folded forward at her waist, flopped over the man's shoulder with a soft thud.

He gasped at the weight of her, of it all. He smoothed her skirt over her backside and then, gripping her legs, carried her out of the barn, her arms flailing, head bobbing with each step, the remaining length of rope trailing behind them—a wedding train dragging dirt and debris from the barn floor on the procession out. Her first marriage till death; her second to Death.

They laid her body on a stretcher and wheeled her bumpily over the gravel path to the ambulance. One of the dogs tried to jump into the back with the body—with her—but the men pushed it out, slammed the door shut in its face. Without saying another word to me, they turned around and drove back up the gravel path, no siren, no flashing lights. Rescued late, the only way she thought she could ever leave this place.

The dogs chased after them. I'm not sure how far the dogs followed but far enough into the distance that I couldn't see them any more. I turned back to the barn. I began to close the doors when my eyes fell on the cow in the corner once more. Given the state of the husband, I had no idea when someone would be over here again to tend to it, and I didn't want to close her up in the barn, stuck and helpless, a second death sentence.

I went back inside, untied her from the post, pulled her along towards the door. She didn't put up a fight. I brought her into the insulting sunlight, closed the doors behind us, and dropped the rope. No more death—today, at least. I remember her giving a long moo. I can still hear that moo, all these years later. Her udder was full, heavy. I bent down and milked her. I didn't bother looking round for a pail. I'm sure there was one right inside the barn, but that was closed for good. I spilled the milk onto the dirt. I just wanted to relieve the creature of her discomfort, and I knew no one else was going to do it, not for a long while.

And I know she was just a cow, but I had the distinct feeling that she had had a bad day, having just watched her owner die before her big, wet eyes. I had no idea how much a cow can comprehend—probably less than a dog, I'd imagine, but the dogs seemed to understand something was not quite right. So I wanted to play it safe. I finished milking her, gave her a pat on the top of her head, and turned to leave.

About halfway up the path, I heard gravel crunching between my tread. I looked back and saw her walking up behind me. I stopped and waited for her to catch up, and then we slowly made the trek back to my home, side by side.

I tied her up to a post in the backyard and went inside the house. I saw my mother glance out the window as she cleaned dishes in the kitchen sink, pausing momentarily as she registered the foreign animal in her yard, but she said nothing. My father didn't mention the cow either. She was our cow now. My cow. I'm the only one who ever took care of her, spent any time with her. For the first couple of weeks, I called her "cow." I eventually came to call her Dove—because she was as sweet and as quiet and as gentle as a dove—but this was just between her and me. To everyone else, she was just the cow.

After that day at the barn, she never did moo again—well, except for once more, but that was much later. And after that day at the barn, I realized I had to get out of there, that I had to work and work hard to get out. I started taking my classes seriously. I stopped talking back to my dad as much. I did my chores in the morning, went to school, came home and did more chores, studied, and went to bed. And I spent my free time with my cow, my Dove. In the summer, I sat by Dove till late in the evening, reading till the dimming light made it impossible to make out the small print on the yellowing pages of the books I nicked off my sister's bookshelf. Sometimes those two dogs of the neighbor's would find us sitting under the same lonely tree alongside the endless fields of corn surrounding our house and would lay beside us and accompany us on our walk back to the old farm house jutting up from the flat fields.

When I finally graduated and left for the Academy, I didn't bother to say goodbye to my parents, and my sister had already left a couple years before for a fancy, expensive university by that point. I tried to explain as best as I could to Dove, though, that I wasn't abandoning her, that I had to go away but would come back for her, rescue her. Since you never know how much animals can understand, I wanted to play it safe. As I swung my duffle back over my shoulder, wearing my uniform, walking up the path to hitch a ride, I heard her give a long moo—her last moo. I felt it in my chest, felt it churn the insides of my gut and try to work its way up my throat in a sob. But, I had to go—I wasn't gonna be rescued late.

A few months later, I received a letter from my mother—the first time my parents had contacted me since I had left—saying that the cow had died. She wrote that my father had dug a grave for her under "that tree I spent so much darn time reading under," that he had lined the plot with stones, that he had mentioned planting flowers there in the spring. She said he left a plaque there, inscribed "Dove," if I ever had an itchin' to stop by one day and see. I'd be able to find it pretty easy, she said.

I remember feeling incredibly thankful. That is, thankful to be alone in my bunk at the time I was reading the letter as tears filled my eyes, spilled down my cheeks. I took several ragged breaths, trying to control myself, control the grief that wrapped around my neck like a noose—a noose dangling from a beam in an old red barn surrounded by fields of corn, shouldering the weight of the heavy blue sky. I even slapped myself across the face, hard. I wiped the blood from my nose with the back of my hand. And there was barking, I remember. Two dogs barking and yapping in my ear, frenzied. Shhh, there's nothing we can do now, I whispered to them. Dove was gone. And, what's more, I had no idea my father knew that I used to spend "so much darn time reading" under that tree with her, that he knew how much I loved the cow—my cow, my Dove—or that he even knew her name. And I had no idea that he cared so much to bury her, to plant flowers, to make a plaque. That he cared so much about me. ◆

JULIE MARIE WADE

GERI DIGIORNO MULTI-GENRE PRIZE CO-WINNER

THIRTEEN WAYS OF LOOKING AT A STONE FRUIT

I

Peechee folders, like my father
carried to class, precursor to his briefcase
in a shade more dust than gold.

Surely, he told someone
I'm just peachy
or even *peachy keen*

with the cowlicked ardor of a sitcom boy.

II

My mother practiced canning
fruits & plans.

If she buried the stones,
they never grew.

Fruitless her garden.

III

Oh, to come from a flower with
superior ovaries!

In health class we memorized
the cow-faced diagram.

I thought they were ears

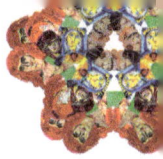

Later, a classmate died
from cancer they failed
to find there.

I hadn't been listening

Before that, long before,
my mother, tumored
& young, survived.

IV

They're *drupes,* not *dupes!*
How buoyantly the cherries
occupy their bowl,

red-red & damasked red-&-gold.

Not drooping those drupes
but *posing—*
still life
with metaphor.

V

I do not know which to prefer,
the apricot dried & mixed for the trail

or the nectarine naked & nearly white,
no fuzz to speak of.

(It's decided! Who could kiss such a blatant lip!)

VI

And yet: *somatic mutation of a normal peach.*

I conjure it up again, call it back—
Peach-freak, be mine!

VII

Remember *The House on Mango Street* in American Lit?
Remember The Peach Pit on *90210?*
Remember the church sign *Forbidden fruits create many jams?*

VIII

When a girl is likened to fruit,
she's sweet, *she's a peach!,* he
shouldn't be *lychee* around her.

When a boy is likened to fruit,
it isn't sweet at all.

It's how your father says *figgy*
but means something else.

It's how your mother loves
Liberace, then suddenly doesn't.

IX

*In some places, they can still
stone you for being a fruit.*
Euphemisms die hard
in the small suburbs.

Fruit, meet punch.
Punch, meet glove.
No daughter of ours is going to be a pugilist!

Some yearnings
take years to bear fruit.

POW!

X

Add a B to every plan
& likewise every plum.

Become the plumber
of the story
on the underside.

Invert it!

The root of the plum is a tree.
The root of the word is a plume.

This is just to say, or really to pen,
that in my early teens,
I barely ate anything.

XI

At some point, the plum
became synonymous with
serendipity:

plum luck that wouldn't dry up,
that refused to prune.

In a college cafeteria,
I scooped them onto my plate.

Feeling stuck? A little backed up?
I didn't know what the mockers meant.

Weren't these wrinkled lumps really
just enormous raisins?

XII

Insatiable & starving,
I learned to hide my appetites
with a fierce aplomb.

XIII

All day it was night.
The moon a coconut
that wouldn't crack.
My heart an olive
pitted against me.

Then, she
suggested
a date.

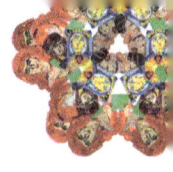

"Some yearnings take years to bear fruit"

— from *"Thirteen Ways of Looking at a Stone Fruit "* by Julie Marie Wade

HAIBUNNY

Long ears, soft pinna, the better to hear you with, my dears. Haibunny thrives on sound, slant rhymes, dines on a steady diet of prosodic grass. Wind-tickled, sun-blanched, those blades. Ever-chewing. Ever-chomping. Haibunny's nothing if not ruminative. Haibunny's nose is a metronome. Haibunny's hocks, muscled onomatopoetically. No mere cryptid, sightings often occur in the wild, but also in the schoolyard, *in the dooryard fronting an old farm-house*, lilacs with heart-shaped leaves happily devoured. Likewise, the hay, which you thought was only for horses. Haibunny can be punny, too. Haibunny can be bale-ful—*get it*—a bale full of hay! Haibunny has been known to wander into church basements, to lick ice cream cups clean & pluck "Peter Peter Pumpkin Eater" on spindly upright pianos. Haibunny eats pumpkins, too, especially relishes the pith. Haibunny plays bingo with your grandmother on Saturday night, calls out *Bash-ō!* every time he wins. Haibunny's tail is a fluffy tuft of assonance, a furtive twitch of consonance. Haibunny, to some, is a metaphor, drawing them down another rabbit hole. Haibunny pals around with Sasquatch & Yeti, Skunk Ape & Yowie, provides composition books & Ticonderogas for all their travelogues. Even Nessie keeps a water-proof diary now. Haibunny is always festival-adjacent, always holiday-aware. Haibunny wears aware well. In fact, Haibunny goes as Harvey for Halloween every year. (You can't see him, but you know he's there.) If you whistle, Haibunny will come hopping. Watch the grasses bend in his wake. If you sing, Haibunny will volunteer to play cowbell in your band. Some legends suggest Haibunny springs into spring every year, bearing bright woven baskets & piebald eggs. Truth is, Haibunny wouldn't want to infringe on another bunny's celebrity. He's modest as a lullaby, descended from the moon. But you'll know he's paid a visit when you crack an egg & find his tiny scroll:

more than four hundred
years of fine poetic lore
in one sweet warren

FRANK CAPRA IS FULL OF SHIT, BUT I'LL LOVE *IT'S A WONDERFUL LIFE!* FOREVER

YOU COULD CALL IT a paean to post-War capitalism—and you wouldn't be wrong. A Truman-era predecessor to GoFundMe—also accurate. Eight thousand. Remember that sum. It's how much money our Everyman needs to raise before this fateful night is done. He'll raise it, too, in hatfuls of crumpled cash, then be christened "the richest man in town" before the final credits roll. His wealth is multivalent, though, not just dollars and cents, but also kith and kin. "No man is a failure who has friends," the newest one reminds him by text (some multivalence here!), especially friends who come heaven-sent and those who organize their own kind of Kickstarter campaign.

You could call it a cautionary tale about suicide—and you wouldn't be wrong. A dramatization of that fabled Dark Night of the Soul—

ditto. An intervention even, with Judeo-Christian overtones and a whiff of "The Serenity Prayer." It soon amused me growing up that our ritual Christmas viewing centered on a man resolved to kill himself. Uplifting, no? Yet somehow yes, it was, & queerly so—the way the camera zoomed perilously close to his face for all the crucial scenes, lines bellowed fog-horn deep while the musical score swelled tsunami-strong. "But George, they'll vote with Potter otherwise." Dun-Dun-DUN! His bottom lip quivering, sweat dripping from the crease in his brow. A film as subtle as a blizzard, I'd say, but the fact is, most people love snow, at least when it's well-timed with their favorite holiday. I'm no exception.

Perhaps you're looking for an old-fashioned love story between a man who doesn't "want to get married, ever, to anyone" and a woman who only wants to marry him. Match made in. . .dare I say it? They pledge their troth during the darkest days of the Great Depression (more multi-valence here!). Two thousand. Remember that sum. It's how much money our Everyman has managed to save—first to travel alone, then to honeymoon together. He hands it to his new wife, that thick stack of bills, in the back of a taxi cab. Only moments later, she'll hand it back to him. In one day, they stop a run on the bank, save the Building & Loan, then spend their wedding night in a water-logged house that should be, if it isn't already, condemned.

You could call it a cinematic parable of Be Careful What You Wish For—and you wouldn't be wrong. Mary broke a window in that decrepit place and wished to live in it one day. George stood on a bridge in a storm and wished he had never been born. Cue here the ultimate subjunctive waltz—or Charleston, as the director clearly prefers. Imagine you've been given a chance to see what the world would be like without you. I'm in it for this proposition precisely. What if my parents had never met at the Sears Roebuck & Company in 1963? Or what if their years of trying for a child had ended like an hourglass that simply sputtered out of sand?

I don't presume I'm special enough to have saved them from each other or themselves, so I like to imagine what blessings might arise from

my absence. "Lasso the moon or lasso the stork—you can't have it both ways," I'd say. Not all librarians are spinsters, of course, and not all spinsters are lonely and sad. (In fact, I'd wager a whole eight grand that more wives lay claim to these conditions than single women can. . .) Perhaps a dangerous property ought to be torn down. Perhaps a scoop of chocolate ice cream served without coconut because, after all, that's what the patron asked for. But those petals, alas—you can't paste them back on the rose. ◆

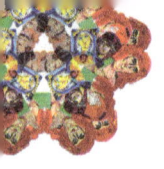

ELLEN KOMBIYIL
GERI DIGIORNO MULTI-GENRE PRIZE CO-WINNER

TRANSLATION

It starts in the middle of the night. You, suddenly awake beneath the ceiling
fan's swirling. A coverlet flutters above you like someone—

your mother—is making the bed with you in it. It flutters like angel wings:
almost translucent. There is no sound. You are a series of impressions. No

mind yet. The moon peeks through the space between window shades; your eyes
adjust to the gleam. Tarantulas slowly climb the cream fabric, or the shadows

of tarantulas. They pattern like leaves rustling—diaphanous spots.
It's happening again. You try to breathe but you cannot. The body begins

to sweat. You are standing now but lying flat on the bathroom tiles.
You want to flee. The fluttering has vanished. Your feet paddling like dogs

run away in their sleep, pursued or pursuing, whimpering. Your husband's voice
beneath you, the warm fuzz of carpet. Your therapist says she thinks "dis-

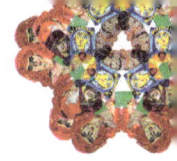

oriented" means you don't know where you are in time and place. "No, I am confused," you say, "about why I have woken in this alien body with no context." When you first

touched a snake, you thought it would be slimy, like a worm uncovered in the dirt, but it was dry, almost rustled at your touch. Your therapist says, "I have never suffered

a migraine." Like a liquid swallowed too quick, you can trace her words down the maw of your throat. Given the chance, you'd swallow the world. But it's the moon

caught mid-gullet. You say this out loud, a kind of translation. Your therapist smiles. It dazzles, how white her teeth, how pretty. Her smile is the edge of the moon.

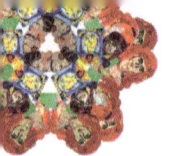

SQUAD TACTICS AS EQUATIONS DEPICTING LOSS

an erasure from Guidebook for Marines, 1954

Chapter 26
Equations Depicting Loss

a   )

When   a   body

        moves   the   body

is

an azimuth, or

                changed

        interval

                of

distance from
                man

                to   man .

b)

        at

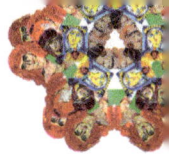

the edge of

woods
                —

                            from the
far edge
            halts   again
                            man

                    one of

    many   possible

            points   .

                            c   )
                    how many
        weapons
            etc.

                    woods, etc.

            are   .

        desirable

                            for

            a   ratio

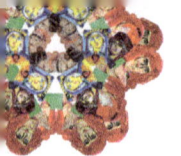

of

oops

of   Maximum

oops

d)

                              no
casual   excess

This :

                    adjacent

                                        men
                  hip
        to

        hip

                                        in
concurrent   sequence

                overrun

                us

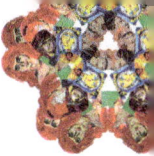

e   )

The

Limit   of

the

                                        self

        :

            each

            particular

                                                assumption

                                        is

                                                        w ere

time   not a factor,

            lost

ADVANCE GUARD

Fig. 26.1 RATE OF "SURVIVAL" AS A FUNCTION OF ADVANCE AND REAR GUARDS ENCIRCLING THE ENEMY

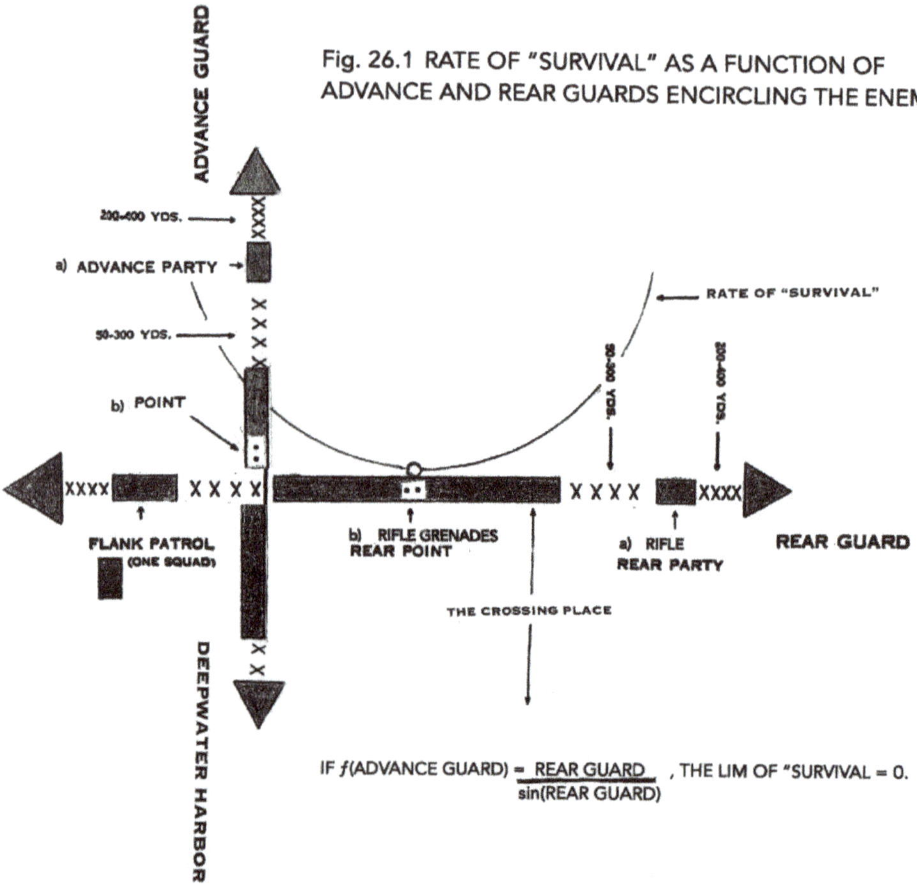

200–400 YDS.

a) ADVANCE PARTY → XXXX

RATE OF "SURVIVAL"

50-300 YDS. X X X X

b) POINT

XXXX   X X X X   X X X X   XXXX

↑   50-300 YDS.   200-400 YDS.

FLANK PATROL
(ONE SQUAD)

b) RIFLE GRENADES
REAR POINT

a) RIFLE
REAR PARTY

REAR GUARD

THE CROSSING PLACE

DEEPWATER HARBOR

X X

IF $f(\text{ADVANCE GUARD}) = \dfrac{\text{REAR GUARD}}{\sin(\text{REAR GUARD})}$, THE LIM OF "SURVIVAL = 0.

MILLIE TULLIS

OUR SIXTH-GRADE BAND TEACHER SOLD HIS OWN CDS AT OUR CONCERTS.

Just five bucks. Just loved
music. Loved the clarinet.
Loved Jimi Hendrix.
One afternoon,
hungover/sick/tired,
he turned off the lights
and turned on
a Jimi Hendrix
concert VHS.
It ended on
"Wild Thing."
"Wild Thing" ended
with Hendrix humping
then smashing
his guitar. Like
the music he'd made
came out so fucking
sweet, he had to
destroy the tools.
Start over. Or
maybe our teacher
fast-forwarded through
the humping/smashing—
was there burning?
But if our teacher did
this, the scene
skipped over
was so obvious,
so unavoidably interesting,
the sped-up bits of song
we missed grew

only more crucial
for us to discuss,
to uncover. Did we see
Jimi hump and smash
and burn in that dark
room? Did we know
the word *hump?* I
did not know *fuck,*
did not know
why my own trap
door thumped
for the morning after
scene in *Romeo + Juliet.*
Probably braver kids,
probably boys,
found it later
on YouTube
and we—girls—
listened to
their memories.
We shouldn't
talk about this.
Precisely the kind
of thing I would
have said. Which
this were we
burying? A
girl is always
burying something.

ESSAY ON LOVE

Ann Bassett was cremated in 1956. Asked for ash to be spread near home. But Frank drove around the ashes til 63. Shared the long leather bench of his pick-up. Spoke to her softly. All the little. All the little nothings you say driving your town, your roads, your mountains. Food and clouds. Cattle and snowfall. The rest of his life.

"Shared the long leather bench of his pick-up. Spoke to her softly."

— from *"Essay on Love"* by Millie Tullis

SINGING LESSONS

I've forgotten more

than I remembered
of this education.

The lessons were held
in her house,

in her basement.
I open the door,

I walk down
dark stairs.

If the other girl
is still

singing, I wait
outside the door.

The door is white.
The wall is white.

I lean against them
and weigh

my voice
against hers.

The basement
smells old

but isn't.
I enter

on time.
My teacher

at the keyboard.
I stand.

Her hands
my mouth

read from the same paper.

BRIAN THOMPSON

TOMMY JACK

THE FIRST TIME Tommy Jack got run over, he'd been a Vernon Parish deputy almost three years. Early that morning, like all his mornings on duty, he stopped at the Citgo U-Pak-It on the south side of Leesville to fill up his unit and grab one of those banana pudding pies he liked for breakfast. On his way out, he spotted the suspect. Skinny guy, hair winging out from under his ball cap, shambling across the gravel parking lot of Broken Promises, the twenty-four-hour dive bar catty-corner to the gas station. Headed for a lifted F-150 with a set of big ass aftermarket tires. Tommy Jack checked his watch. 7:36.

He tossed his pudding pie into the passenger seat of his unit and proceeded across the road. The suspect climbed into the cab of a pickup, hoisting himself maybe four feet or so off the gravel. He still had his driver's side door open when Tommy Jack hopped the ditch separating the Broken Promises parking lot from the street.

He called out, "Sir, you got somewhere to be so early?"

"Buddy, I got everywhere to be," the suspect said.

Tommy Jack didn't know what that meant. "Wanna let me know about how much you've had to drink this morning?"

The suspect was uncooperative. He put his key in the ignition and started to close his door. Tommy Jack could cut him loose. Let the guy peel out, flinging rocks every which way. Let him swerve on down the highway till he smashed into a mailbox or pancaked a schoolkid.

Instead, Tommy Jack made two big strides and leapt at the truck. He figured maybe he'd get enough air to grab hold of the suspect's jeans and rip the guy out of the cab on his way to the ground. Too late, he saw the grease sheen on the denim. This guy must have worked graveyard at the paper mill, trudging around in that oily air. Tommy Jack's grip slipped loose. He ended up flat on the gravel with his arms stretched in front of him like Superman. The suspect ran over his hands.

They sunk into the rock a bit, which took some of the pressure off, thank goodness. He was lucky not to find a couple stumps at the ends of his arms. Instead, he suffered fractures to both metacarpals (thumb bones), his left proximal phalanx (pointer finger bone), and a couple-other bones he couldn't read from the crappy PDF scan on his online insurance portal.

As he lay there in the Broken Promises parking lot, Tommy Jack watched the suspect drift onto the road calm as anything, those big ass tires barely launching a pebble. He proceeded a couple few blocks down the way, never veering outside the lines, until he pulled under the aluminum carport of a brick ranch style with an old TV antenna forking out of the roof.

He didn't serve any time. Didn't even get booked. Sheriff Robicheaux said he couldn't have done much harm drunk driving when he lived so close to Broken Promises.

"If they don't smell too bad and they're within half a mile of home," she told Tommy Jack in her Cajun drawl, "I just let 'em go with God. Did he stink of booze?"

Tommy Jack looked at the TV hung up in the corner of his hospital room, thinking. The fuzzy picture showed a Cialis commercial where a guy and a lady kissed in a photo booth. "Happened too quick to get a whiff," Tommy Jack said.

The doctors wrapped both his hands in chunky white casts like plaster mittens and sent him on home. The department gave him a month of paid leave. After his mama passed, just before the sheriff hired him, he'd moved into his mama's old trailer back in the woods off Old Sterlington Road. Just a single wide, but the property stretched for a couple hundred acres. He'd grown fond of the lifestyle. In his duplex in town, he'd all the time have to sleep with his head sandwiched between two pillows on account of the tweakers banging around on the other side of the wall. Out here it was quiet. In the summer, he hung hummingbird feeders from the trees and sat in his lawn chair with a Diet Dr. Pepper, watching the buggers buzz around. He even had his own pond. And if he wanted to, he could go outside in the middle of the night and scream his head off. There wasn't a soul around to care.

TOMMY JACK sat in front of the TV having a pizza roll dinner. After a few nights of struggle, he figured out how to pinch a roll between his plaster mittens and suck it into his mouth. During Blue Bloods, they showed a commercial for a Disney beach resort in Hawaii. He never cared for Disney stuff growing up. His mama wouldn't let him watch it anyway. At church, they told everyone not to let your kids watch Disney for all the subliminal messages. Apparently there was a part in The Great Mouse Detective where you could pause the tape and see the mouse's penis.

On the commercial, a family rode what looked like big floating tricycles out on the ocean. They had huge plastic wheels in pastel colors with treads running straight across that served as paddles. Tommy Jack pictured himself riding one of those tricycles in his pond. The pond was big around as a Walmart. Plenty of room to putter. He could sit back and let his legs pump. Give his injured hands a rest. Plus, it'd be better exercise than sitting in front of the TV all the time. He could put it on his Mastercard.

With one mitten, he held his phone steady on his TV tray and pressed the tip of his other mitten to the side button. He told Siri to search for those big tricycles you can ride on water. She looked around and found out they're called Aqua-Cycles. They come in all kinds of configurations.

Two-seaters, one-seaters. Different color wheels. Tommy Jack had Siri call their 800 number, and he ordered himself a standard one-seater with the regular blue and yellow wheels. It came to almost five grand after tax. Free shipping, though.

The Aqua-Cycle arrived at the trailer in a refrigerator-sized box, plus the wheels done up in plastic wrap. It had to sit in the grass for half a week. Tommy Jack couldn't put it together with his mittens on, and his son Andrew couldn't get off work at Burger King until Friday. Andrew had worked his way up to evening manager in only a couple years. Tommy Jack didn't see him much when the kid was growing up. Andrew spent most of his life in Houston with his mother. He moved to Leesville after high school so he could work on an oil rig offshore, but he didn't like it too much. Burger King was meant to be temporary, but he took to it. Tommy Jack liked having Andrew nearby. Turned out they were both big fans of Ed McBain mysteries and even turned each other on to a few they'd overlooked. Sometimes they'd be sitting out back of the trailer, wagging their chins, and Tommy Jack wished he and Andrew'd come out here when mama was still alive. Hell, he wished he'd come out more often, even just by himself.

"You want me to push her out to the pond?" Andrew asked when he'd finished putting the tricycle together.

Tommy Jack leaned on the splintery porch railing. He'd set out some citronella candles to keep the mosquitoes away while Andrew worked, but he still found a red bump on his neck to itch. "Sure, wheel her on out there," he said.

Andrew lifted his dirty suede work glove to his forehead and gave his daddy a two-fingered salute. Tommy Jack followed him as he rolled the Aqua-Cycle to the pond. Its wheel paddles made three tracks of horizontal lines in the dirt. Andrew eased it into the black water.

"You got any rope or a bungie or something I can tie her off with?"

"I think I'd like to try her out a while first," Tommy Jack said.

"You sure? Can't hardly see a thing out here in the dark."

Tommy Jack's phone hung from a lanyard around his neck. He pressed the side button and said, "Siri, turn on my flashlight." Sure enough, she did. He pinched the phone between his mittens and shined the light on the Aqua-Cycle, then at Andrew. "I'll be all right."

"Okay, well, let me help you up on it."

Andrew held the tricycle steady with one hand and took one of his daddy's mittens in the other. Tommy Jack had to wade into the water a bit to reach the step bar. He hooked his other mitten through a hole in the back of the plastic seat and pulled himself up. The Aqua-Cycle didn't wobble too much. Tommy Jack plopped onto the seat right where it had a ridge to go between the butt cheeks. Real comfortable, he thought. He set his feet on the pedals and churned them backward.

"Here I go," he said.

Andrew gave the Aqua-Cycle a push, and the next thing either of them knew Tommy Jack was out on the pond, pumping away.

"I can't see you out there," Andrew called out. "You okay?"

Tommy Jack turned his phone's flashlight back on and waved it around. "Doing great!"

"Shoot, you should've got a beer before you went out there. Want me to toss you one?"

"Don't think I could catch it," Tommy Jack called out.

"Okay, well, I'm heading out then. You be careful. Ain't safe on the pond by yourself."

Tommy Jack ignored that last bit. Andrew had some funny ideas about the pond. He waved to his son, but he couldn't see if Andrew waved back. He watched him get in his old rusted pickup, the one he bought with his signing bonus from the oil company. Under the dome light, Andrew cracked open a Michelob Ultra and took a swig before heading off down the long, rutted driveway. That boy could throw back six or seven of those and still be sober as a deacon.

Pretty soon, Tommy Jack lost sight of Andrew's taillights through the trees along Old Sterlington. He stopped pedaling and let the Aqua-Cycle drift wherever she wanted. He thought maybe he heard some gunshots from whatever show he'd left on in the trailer. He crossed his mittens over the handlebars, leaned his cheek against the cool plaster, and dozed off.

When he woke up, the Aqua-Cycle had lodged itself against the bank. The reeds growing up from the shallow water at the edge clicked against the hollow plastic of the front wheel. Tommy Jack lifted his head off the handlebars, feeling an awful crick in his neck. Thank goodness the sun hadn't been up long enough to burn him. He turned his head this way and that, as far as it would go on either side, hoping to work out the knot. That's when he saw the dead woman, way out on the south side of the pond.

She lay on her stomach with her feet on the grassy bank and her face submerged in the shallow water. She was far enough away that Tommy Jack couldn't make out every detail. She looked about five and a half feet tall. Sickly skinny. She had ivory-colored skin. Like real ivory. Yellowed as old piano keys. Clumps of greasy gray hair floated around her head. She was totally nude, poor thing. A white egret stood on top of her with its beak tucked under its wing, picking away at something. It perched on a bony peak of one of the woman's butt cheeks. He'd never seen this woman before. The closest neighbors were five miles off, a family of soybean farmers called the Dews. Maybe they had a granny who'd wandered over to Tommy Jack's property in a fit of dementia. It would've been the first he'd heard of such a lady, but some families kept folks like that a secret. Then again, there's no way a skinny old woman like that could trudge across miles of soybean fields and creek beds and drainage ditches and acres and acres of nettles.

Tommy Jack hooked his mittens over the handles of the Aqua-Cycle and pumped the pedals backward, easing off the bank. He cut the front wheel hard to the right and swung the tricycle around toward the far shore. He didn't pedal hard. Not too eager for a closer look. He knew water could do all sorts of nasty things to a body. The Aqua-Cycle floated over slow as a baby's first steps.

Halfway there, maybe a little less, he slipped his feet off the pedals and let the Aqua-Cycle drift. The bird unsettled him. He was pretty sure egrets fed on bugs and little critters like that. He'd seen one fish a worm from the rotten bark of a fallen cypress tree. But now he had a notion this egret would any second unsheathe its beak from its wing and slice into the dead woman's back. He felt it in his gut. This bird would pluck some sticky strip of offal from between her ribs, fling it into the air with a flick of its curved neck, and catch the morsel in its open mouth.

He called out, "Skedaddle!"

The egret launched from its perch. Tommy Jack ducked under his mittens, just in time to hear a claw scrape across the plaster. He screamed, but no one could hear him out there.

And when he raised his head, the woman in the water was gone.

THEY CUT HIS MITTENS OFF on a Wednesday afternoon. He could use his hands pretty good by then. Just had a bit of an ache when he made a fist. Sheriff Robicheaux put him back on morning patrol.

"Try not to get run over, hear?" she said.

She grinned at Tommy Jack, and he grinned back.

He went to the Citgo U-Pak-It to pick up a banana pudding pie and a Diet Dr. Pepper. He glanced across the way at Broken Promises but didn't see any DUI suspects in the parking lot.

Could be someone inside waiting to come out, but if they wanted to nest there behind those blackened windows and drink the morning away, Tommy Jack figured they could go ahead. You had a right to sit in the bar and pickle your liver all you wanted in Vernon Parish, long as it wasn't a Sunday.

He took a loop around the paper mill and drove by the Haywood apartments next to the Sam's Club. He'd every now and then stumble across some narcotics activity or domestic disturbances over there, but not today. He pulled into the strip mall on White's Ferry Road and parked his unit in a spot without too many weeds growing through the blacktop. He opened his pudding pie and doodled in his notepad.

Tommy Jack had been a doodler since forever. When he was a boy, his mama used to cut up those flat business card magnets they handed out at the oil change place and use the strips to stick his doodles on the fridge. She once sent away for a drawing test where he had to choose either to copy a realistic picture of a pirate's head or a cartoony picture of a turtle wearing a floppy newsboy cap. Tommy Jack chose the turtle, since he'd learned to doodle in the first place by tracing Ninja Turtles off his Trapper Keeper. His copy turned out pretty good. His mama sent the test off, but she got a letter back saying he was too young for their art school and to try again when he turned eighteen. He never did.

He doodled in his notepad a picture of a hand wrapped up in a plaster mitten. On another page, he tried to draw the Aqua-Cycle from memory, but the proportions looked funny. He flipped the page again. Sort of half thinking about it, he drew a couple of long, squiggly lines. He kept going and kept going, and the next thing he knew he had a picture of the woman in the pond. He hadn't intended to draw her when he put pencil to paper, but he carried on all the same. And though his natural inclination when it came to doodling tended toward the cartoony, he found himself squiggling in every crease and cranny he could remember of that old lady's naked frame. He couldn't draw hands too good, so he kept them hidden underwater. He made two tiny Vs for the points of her butt. He left out the bird.

Something caught the corner of his eye. A suspicious gentleman crossing the parking lot. Late middle age, about five nine. Black hair, gray at the temples. Mustache. Stocky build. Wearing a blue, short-sleeve button-down and light blue jeans. No visible tattoos.

Tommy Jack checked his watch. 7:23 in the morning. None of the stores in the strip mall were open. He scanned the signs. A nail salon. Sherwin-Williams. A check cashing place. H&R Block. A pet shop called Tailwaggers.

He brushed pudding pie crumbs off his chest and sat up in the driver's seat of his unit.

The suspicious gentleman walked along the front of the strip mall with a slight hunch. Either he didn't see Tommy Jack or he didn't care about a police unit sitting fifty feet away. He stopped in front of Tailwaggers and pressed his face against the window. They had a square of AstroTurf on the other side of the glass with a white picket fence around it. The dogs that got dropped off for daycare would play on the fake grass and get ogled by passersby. Today's doggies hadn't shown up yet. It was dark inside. The suspicious gentleman cupped both hands around his eyes to get a better look through the glass, then headed around the side of the strip mall and out of Tommy Jack's sight. Experienced burglars don't always hit the kind of places you might expect. For example, it's nearly impossible to rob a bank and get away with it these days. And if you knock over a liquor store, there's a good chance you'll get a face full of buckshot.

Sometimes places like a Tailwaggers keep a safe in the back. The people who work there don't worry about robberies, so they're lazy about bank runs. They can rack up a lot of cash. Tommy Jack thought back to Pearl, the little Shih Tzu he and his ex had before Andrew was born. Her grooming cost an arm and a leg, and that was over twenty years ago. No telling what kind of fortune could be in the back of Tailwaggers.

He slipped his nightstick from his belt loop and eased out of his unit, careful not to bang the door shut too loud. No sign of the suspect around the side of the strip mall. He couldn't have gone out to the road. Tommy Jack would've seen him. He must have proceeded behind the building, hoping to gain entry through a back door.

Tommy Jack inched around the corner with his back pressed against the cinderblock. He returned his nightstick to his belt and pulled his G22, though he kept the safety on. Not once had he discharged his sidearm on duty, and he had a mind to keep it that way. A record like that means an officer knows how to use his head.

Here and there, metal awnings hung over the back doors to the businesses. Some of the doors had latches with padlocks. Others, like the door to Tailwaggers, had a keyhole. The suspect must have gained entry already. Maybe he picked the lock. Or maybe he had a key. Inside job? Either way, Tommy Jack held his service pistol ready in his left hand. He balled up the newly healed fingers of his right and pounded on the door.

"Sheriff's Department! Anyone in there?"

Nothing. He tried the knob, and the door clicked open. The dummy forgot to lock it behind him. Tommy Jack eased it out of the jamb and peeked inside. The back room of Tailwaggers was pitch black.

"I'm coming in! I don't wanna have to shoot nobody!"

Still nothing. He could have swung the door open, tried to flood the room with sunlight. But the suspect might land a couple rounds in Tommy Jack's chest from behind a carton of Alpo or wherever he might be hiding. Instead, Tommy Jack pulled the door just wide enough to squeeze inside and shut it behind him. He crouched, making himself a smaller target. He felt the wall above him for a light switch. No luck. In the strip of sunlight leaking under the door, he could make out the edges of a metal shelving unit against the wall beside him. He felt along its length and paced heel-to-toe deeper into the shadows, ready for anything.

He heard a wooden snap under his foot. Something in the darkness coiled around his ankles like a slap bracelet. He bent down to feel it. Chicken wire? He'd walked into a booby trap. Tommy Jack tried to take a step, but his bound-up feet wouldn't budge. He hopped a bit, then timbered head-first into a bucket of water. No, not water. Whatever it was, it burned like hell. It stung inside his nostrils and down the back of his throat. He tipped the bucket over trying to pull himself to his knees. The liquid spread across the concrete floor and soaked into his shirt. His lungs burned when he breathed. He grabbed the radio clipped to his shoulder and brought it to his lips, but all that came out of his mouth was vomit.

He kept his eyes squeezed shut against the burning liquid. Bad enough having broken his hands in the line of duty. He wasn't about to go blind. He pawed at the chicken wire, but it held fast. He had to get away from this puddle of poison. He grabbed for the metal shelf, found it, and pulled himself to his feet. He hopped back to the door and yanked it wide. The sunlight shined through his eyelids with a reddish tint.

He remembered a trickle of a ditch running through the empty lot beside the strip mall. Muddy water, for sure. Maybe even some raw sewage in there. But he had to wash his eyes out, sewage or no. Worst case, he'd need a couple shots.

He made a couple hops away from the door and felt something like a wasp sting on his left bicep, sending him spinning on his wired-up heels. The pet robber popped him, that son of a bitch. Tommy Jack dropped to the blacktop.

THEY KEPT HIM IN ST. FRANCIS a couple days. There'd been a chicken wire puppy pen set up in the back of Tailwaggers, and he'd stepped on one of the wooden dowels propping it up. His legs happened to be in the way when it tried to re-coil itself. He thanked God there were no puppies in the pen, or that whipping wire might've taken one of their eyes. The puppies had been cleared out so Tailwaggers could do their regular deep cleaning. Otherwise they never would've left a bucket of bleach sitting around.

Tommy Jack also thanked God he hadn't been shot in the arm. The owner of the check cashing place parked in the back of the strip mall every morning. He'd rounded the corner and clipped Tommy Jack with the side mirror of his Ford Fiesta. Not his fault. Who could have guessed there'd be a deputy hopping around back there? Tommy Jack made a mental note to send the guy some flowers for calling the ambulance.

"How you feeling, Tommy Jack?" Sheriff Robicheaux said.

She'd brought him a tin of butter cookies and a bottle of Diet Dr. Pepper from the machine in the waiting room. He told her there was a footrest she could pop out of the chair where she sat by his hospital bed, but she didn't partake. She sat real stiff and every now and then fiddled with the fuzzy elastic she used to hold her ponytail back. She always had that thing tied so tight her hair looked like orange streaks painted right on her skull.

"My face and my neck are still tender from where the bleach got on 'em," Tommy Jack said. "And the cuts on my ankles're still itching me some. Got a nasty bruise on my bicep. But those drops they gave me help a lot with my eyes."

"You look pretty pink."

"Yeah, they said I'll be pink for a while. They're gonna x-ray my lungs tonight. They said I can go home if it turns out clear."

"That's good news," Sheriff Robicheaux said. She rubbed her hands up and down her thick thighs. The calluses on her palms made a quiet scraping sound on the polyester of her uniform pants. "That's good news," she repeated.

Tommy Jack opened the cookie tin sitting on his bed tray. "You want a cookie?"

"Yeah, I'll take one of those round ones."

She did.

"I like the ones with the big sugar crystals on top," Tommy Jack said. "Well, tell the truth, I like all of them." He bit one of the ones with the sugar crystals and crunched it around in his mouth. "How's the investigation going?" A puff of crumbs came out when he said it.

Sheriff Robicheaux took a bite of her cookie. "Well, I talked to Tammy down at Tailwaggers, and she said there didn't seem to be anything missing from the shop. That bleach got up under some bags of dog food, so they had to throw those away. And I went ahead and got her some more chicken wire at Lowe's."

"They don't have insurance?"

"It was only twenty-five bucks, Tommy Jack. They don't need to worry about no insurance."

"Guess not," Tommy Jack said. "The insurance man'd probably ask about their back door being unlocked. Probably deny all claims based on that alone."

"Yeah, maybe so. Anyway, I'm glad you're okay. How're your hands treating you?"

Tommy Jack had forgotten the last time he'd walked out of St. Francis, he had a new pair of plaster mittens. He held up both his hands and made fists. "Oh, fine," he said.

She nodded and stared at the half cookie still in her hand. "I can't finish this," she said. She lifted her butt off the chair and leaned forward to set the rest of her cookie on the tray table. Before she sat back down, she pulled a piece of folded paper out of her back pocket. With her eyes on the floor, she said, "Tommy Jack, I found this in your unit."

She unfolded the paper. It had a ragged top where she'd torn it out of Tommy Jack's notebook. It was his doodle of the woman in the pond. He felt a hot blush swell up from his neck. It irritated his bleach burns. He itched his cheeks with the nubs of his chewed-off fingernails, then stopped for fear it might turn him even pinker.

"I don't want to embarrass you, Tommy Jack, but I'm glad I found this before any of the other deputies. Can you tell me what it is?"

"Just a doodle."

"It's pretty good. You got some talent."

He picked up the bottle of Diet Dr. Pepper she'd brought him. He twisted the cap, cracking the plastic ring, and could tell from the fizz it was going to spill over. He tightened the cap closed quick as he could, then set the bottle back on the tray. He could hear it still hissing.

"I'm just an old doodler," he said without looking at the sheriff.

She held the picture in both hands and studied it, nodding her head. She raised her eyebrows like she'd just thought of something surprising, then lowered them. She stood up, folded the paper, and slipped it under the cookie tin. She hitched up her pants with a tug on her duty belt. Tommy Jack thought she had a sad air about her now. Either it'd sprung up all of a sudden, or he hadn't noticed it before.

"How you getting along since your mama passed, Tommy Jack?"

He picked up the sheriff's half a cookie and ate it himself.

"Not too bad," he said. "Got myself an Aqua-Cycle."

He realized not everyone probably knows what an Aqua-Cycle is from name alone, but Sheriff Robicheaux didn't ask.

"Your mama didn't look like that when we pulled her from the pond," she said.

"I know she didn't."

"She had on all her clothes, for one."

"I know," Tommy Jack said.

Sheriff Robicheaux had shown him the pictures. She showed them one at a time, only flipping to the next one when he said he was ready.

"I'm gonna have to let you go, Tommy Jack."

She said the department would take real good care of him. She gave him two months' salary, and he didn't even have to come into the station. She told him she'd give him a glowing reference if he wanted to apply back at the mill or wherever else. If she heard something about an opening, she'd be sure to let him know. She said if Tommy Jack ever needed anything, he should give her a call on her personal phone. She looked around for somewhere to write the number and ended up having to do it on the back of his doodle.

Tommy Jack didn't bother applying at the mill. Over the past few years, he'd handed out more than a few tickets to some of his old co-workers there. But it wasn't too long before he found a job running baby trees for Sal Petito. He'd gone over to Petito's Nursery to pick up some herbs, thinking he might want to plant an herb garden behind his trailer. They got to talking, and come to find out Sal was selling a lot more baby trees than he had room for on his premises. Tommy Jack told him he had his mama's hand-me-down pickup and lots of empty land. He could keep the baby trees on his property and run them into town as needed. They worked out a fair price for the service. Enough to keep the lights on, anyway. Plus, he liked having all those baby trees outside. He and Andrew would spend the occasional afternoon sitting on the deck with some beers, admiring them. Like his own little orchard.

It was about 5:00 in the evening when he came upon the wreck. The days were getting shorter, so the sun had already started to set. Tommy Jack saw the road flares the state troopers had set up along the center lane of the Interstate and pulled his pickup onto the shoulder. He had a full load of trees in the back.

An eighteen-wheeler sat tipped on its side in the right-hand lane. A trooper stood by one of the flares, waving traffic through at a slow clip. He had on one of those wide-brimmed trooper hats. Tommy Jack wondered why they never got hats like that at the sheriff's department.

The trooper held up a hand when Tommy Jack got close. "Sir, could you please get back in your vehicle?"

"Tommy Jack Cascio. I used to be a sheriff's deputy. Thought I'd offer y'all a hand if you need it."

State troopers work the Interstate wrecks, but Tommy Jack would help out from time to time if he didn't have anything else going on.

"We've got it under control, sir."

"All right. Well, I'll just hang around in case y'all need some help with the cleanup later." Tommy Jack chuckled. "Got nothing better to do, I guess."

"Sir, for your own safety, I'm gonna have to ask you to please return to your vehicle."

Tommy Jack held up his hands. "All right. If you need me, I'll be in my truck over yonder."

A glint of orange light caught his eye. The Interstate ran along Lake Vernon, and he could see the surface of its brown water sparkling through the treeline by the road, stretching almost to the horizon. The thick sunset glow laid over the lake like a blanket. A cypress tree stood alone out there, far from dry land. Near the top, Tommy Jack could see a white egret perched on a tuft of Spanish moss.

He felt a crawling sensation around his feet, like bugs creeping under his socks. He looked down and found himself standing in an ant bed as big as a pillow. In the flickering pink light of the road flares, he couldn't tell if they were red ants or not, but just about every ant in the state was liable to be a fire ant. Tommy Jack stomped his feet, but it seemed like every stomp brought another swarm of ants out of their den. He grabbed a handful of jeans above each of his knees and pulled his pant legs up, kicking his feet to try and fling the suckers off.

He stomped his way off the shoulder and onto the road. He heard the state trooper yelling from the wreck site, but he couldn't make out what was said. Tommy Jack assumed the trooper was mad he wasn't back in his truck. He looked up to holler at the trooper about the ants on his feet, and that's when the Trans Am hit him.

Tommy Jack always thought Trans Ams were beautiful cars. He liked the black ones with the gold firebirds painted on the hood. They looked so gorgeous with their wings flared around the scoop.

As he rolled across that long hood, he noticed this one didn't have a firebird painted on it. Just plain black. But it did have a scoop. Hurt like hell when it cracked his left femur. By then, he'd rolled so he could see through the windshield. The kid behind the wheel looked about as shocked as Tommy Jack. He was about nineteen or twenty, looked like. Around Andrew's age. He had to've been drinking, or he would have seen the road flares and let off the gas. He braked a bit before he ran into Tommy Jack, but only a bit. Even after the hood scoop took out his leg, Tommy Jack still had plenty of momentum to crack against the windshield and fly up over the roof of that pretty car.

He turned his head toward the lake, now high enough to see over the treeline. The egret had flown from the cypress, and the last of the day's sunlight had melted from orange to purple. And a long ways off, teeny as an ant, Tommy Jack saw the three pastel wheels of his Aqua-Cycle rolling along the water. The naked woman from the pond sat in the driver's seat, her skeletal legs pedaling like crazy.

He thought about calling to her. Maybe asking her who she was. He had the time to do it, floating up in the air with his limbs splayed. Andrew once told him about this place over in Baton Rouge where you can spend an hour at a time in a big tank of salt water. He said they close you in the tank so it's pitch black and you can't hear a thing. In the salt water, you can relax your muscles and float. Not a thought of sinking to the bottom and drowning. Andrew said you get to where you don't think about anything, which is the whole point of the tank. Tommy Jack thought he might want to go someday. But Baton Rouge was pretty far.

◆

SARA DUDO

FLOWER MARKET

In the future, there will be rooms.

At dusk while clouds rupture
I heave flowers into the black hole
of lake water

       [in relativity, a black hole
defined as an expanse of spacetime

in which the gravitational field is so
strong that nothing can escape it.]

A black hole is
a summer offering.

Floating begonias:

gold and peach halfglobes
scattering spheres, a reflection of nimbus rings.

The Sebring sits stuck in deep sand grooves.

Between us and the light, a fermata of yearning
and fable of the windmill still above trees.

       Bullfrogs. Orbweavers. My waist
       closing the seam between water
       and skin:

a seam joins but also closes.

[String theory says everything
is made up of exceptionally tiny strings

whose vibrations produce effects
we interpret as atoms and electrons.]

String theory is my arms
around your neck

traversing day waves
into an accumulation of pinks,
lives into an accumulation of boxes.

BOBBY ELLIOTT

WRITING ROOM

From the only lit room
in the house I listen
to the sound of you

gathering speed
in the hallway,
stumbling towards me

like you're still
dreaming of bucket swings
slicked with rain, already

one of those people
who gets to where
they need to go

a full hour early —
my cup of tea
newly drinkable

and the epistles
of *White Apples*
and the Taste of Stone

just getting good
when I hear
what can only be

you: hurtling, destined
to trip and cry out
in the morning

of the morning,
needing me to come
hold you and sing

with a pen
in my mouth
and an image

evaporating. Instead
you slow down
by the baby gate

and lower yourself
into my writing room
like a child who knows

what they want:
the hole punch
you've just learned

to take apart
and shake, all
the small paper

circles falling out
as you laugh
and call for your

pregnant mother
to join us
in the light.

SHIFTING

I'm shifting my sleep schedule to be up in the blue light,
then the black. Snowstorm this morning—I like to watch
it blow off the rooftops in gusts. I feel like a seal, finally
understanding currents, the way air or water exists not
as a single entity but a series of interlocking chains in
motion. But of course I don't really get it, don't get even
the weather. It's like recently when my great-grandmother

asked me about the internet and I was left fumbling in my
own words. Something is...floating in space? Grandma
has a charming habit of saying, "can you ask Mrs. Google?"
when she suspects the answer is in reach. The hill between us
might after this storm be too snowy to cross, a partial
relief. Listening to her verbally berate my mother this Christmas,
I took the phone in defense. She said "are *you* Melody?" as if

she couldn't remember my name is her own. The blue light
wisps to white and that's daytime. When the wind dies down,
the horizon is currentless, a bunch of lumps falling from space.

BRAD CLOMPUS
DOMESTIC DISPUTE

END OF SUMMER CAMP, sister and I resettled unwarned to new lodgings: a three-tiered blockhouse apartment, hard-edged bleached bricks, plunked in nowhere fringe of city, not our snug house across from edge less woods down the street from farms—where we thought we still lived until this moment. Inside, tableau of parents morphed by divorce, warped into people we couldn't imagine. That letter we found months ago in a kitchen drawer *(irreconcilable...abandonment)* pure gibberish. When they open the door to the freshly painted apartment, distract us with baloney sandwiches, deliver the news straight-faced *(it's not so bad you'll like it here)*, my sister and I act out yin-yang temperaments: she's howling in her assigned room *(let her get it out of her system)*, and I, sanguine stomach-clenched eight-year-old, reassure the nodding heads: *It'll be all right, it'll be nice* ("it" referring to the estranged terrain; "nice" a hypothetical zone of sweetness, of non-harm).

SNOWING, FAINTLY AT FIRST, the kind that adorns your flushed cheeks with perfectly realized flakes. Then it gets serious. Time to dress for school, but forget it, nobody goes to school on such a day. Victory speech on the radio: *All public and parochial schools closed* . . . incorruptible joy lingers beyond breakfast. My sister and me in pajamas, shoulder to shoulder at the living room window, but not too close to the glass— that would fog it blind. We see the long asphalt parking lot behind our blockhouse. Don't know anyone here, not like the street where a skinny old man in a bungalow baked us crumbly gingersnaps; where Miss Manibold in a decrepit mansion shook her fist at the kids' careening shouts, though sometimes served as much sickly-sweet red punch as we could drink; where the Cateer Gang coursed us through the woods like rabbits with shuddering hearts.

But those people down on the lot, they're just wobbling marionettes. Through the gauzy veil of snow, a car idling, blue smoke escaping the tailpipe. A big white sedan, more than ample for the man in overcoat and gloves and jaunty checkered hat who pivots his legs onto the seat, flicks his clumsy galoshed feet through the passenger door yanked open by a woman, *his* woman, who's wearing a thin periwinkle robe and golden slippers, her hair feathery and unkempt, skin powder white, violet lipstick smeared past its limit. She's calling, in an unraveling wail, *puuhleeez* or *poleeece* over and over as she slips on the groundless ground, losing what grip she has while the dirty boots keep pushing.

A REAL HORROR SHOW—though not as good as *The Black Museum* which we watched late one night all by ourselves, where even before the blood-seeping title, the dire horns and strings, a young fancy woman's eyes get needle-pierced by binoculars mailed to her by, what else, a spurned suitor. What wasn't she meant to see? And that other woman, below, on ice—should we call the *poleeece?* No, we shouldn't, we won't. Mom's still asleep, but even awake, she might freeze in place. The woman in the lot now divided in two, upper half propped by elbows on the car seat, the lower kneeling on blacktop, while the slick black boots are ousting her, inch by inch.

But we don't stay around for the wrap-up, because something else calls: our TV puppets, Fussy and Gussy, the bumbling bubbleheads, always chased by the villainous fox, Sir Guy de Guy, always at risk for falling, falling to the Witch in the Well. All danger crests, then resolves in thirty minutes while we chew on brittle flakes crusted with sugar or hollow balls of mush that mimic chocolate. After the show, back at the window, things have changed: snow blustering densely from all directions, layering everything, sheeting the neighborhood, almost erasing it. Makes us giddy, hopeful. We keep staring—but no one else arrives to entertain. Only tire treads printed on the driveway; a chaotic mess of shoe prints, knee holes, leggy skids trailing into slush, like something wild has happened. On the concrete steps that lead to our blockhouse, a gold slipper half-transfigured by snow—fairy tale debris. *Should I get the slipper before it's ruined?* my sister asks. *No, leave it there, her husband will pick it up when he comes home. He'll bring it to her. He'll get on his knees, say he's sorry.* Like that's what he is and that's what he'll do. ◆

ALEJANDRA HERNÁNDEZ

THERE'S GOLD ON THE OTHER SIDE OF THIS MOUNTAIN, WE JUST HAVE TO CROSS THIS BRIDGE FIRST —

Georgie's skeptical but I say I'll bring him home
tomorrow. His blue hoodie has a new patch &
we can make love all night & I will buy him
Mickey D's breakfast if we get there on time.
He wipes on a grin & rolls his eyes. The car
already running, my baby is sleeping inside.
The golden vein of August pans the blue sky,
like a compass that leads, like the north star
that guides. After sundown, we become a sweet
liquid; Chamomile flowers spun open in secret.

ZACHARY LAMALFA

THE BOATS

My dance card is full. I quit.
Goodbye, lords and ladies. I quit.
I raise my hand to hail the
Sailboats permanently turning
Pegs on the same stocks, same
Sound of rocks and water tuning.
My horses always lose. I quit
And set my horses free
To hoof along the beach. An hour with
A beautiful lover or the prince
Of the sea would be enough
But the road is too narrow
The sea is too rough. I quit.
The commandments don't keep.
The house is cold. So I quit
And the house is without ghosts
Without furniture or mice. The mice
Have quit. The ghosts have
Migrated somewhere warmer
A shipwreck or crypt. Some end up
In historical societies. The cities
Keep their ghosts, disburse them
When sailors disembark. Others
End up in museums. Sailors
Have a long and tumultuous history
They keep to themselves in
The observance of their tasks.
I have no tasks and no
History. I work the reeds
At the fringes. I supervise
The men stoking the engine. I quit.

Give me the boats, I quit.
Goodbye, lords and ladies. I was
A mouse in the granary. Then
I was the cat. And the saints
Returning from the sea
After the storm clears
Gather and begin to swap name-
Tags at the walls of the city.

SONG

I am a peasant and the year is 805
I don't know that part, the year
I do know that I'm a peasant
I have no ego, a weariness induced foot cramp
I sleep on a pallet of hay in a muddy cottage
I look at stars through the hole in the roof
  1) the star of priests' whispers
  2) the star of intestinal distress
  3) the star of petty social obligation
  4) the dead star whose dead light will arouse the literate for centuries
But I don't know that part, the centuries
The sky is full of holes
Now it's the year 905
Now it's raining

ROSE REA

VANILLA

1.

My wife died when I was thirty-eight, after a short illness. We'd been married since we were kids, and when she'd gone I felt as if I had only lived about one tenth of the life I'd planned on living. Yes, I was heartbroken. But I was also in a hurry to investigate the space that her dying had opened up.

I stayed out at the One Too Many Saloon until the early morning. Young women visited the One Too Many. They weren't locals. They came from wherever young women come from and lined up to ride the mechanical bull, wearing little jean shorts and even littler shirts that said John Deere, Budweiser. I was still good-looking then. They'd dare each other to slow dance with me after they'd had a few. Once, I asked one of them: what do you want out of life? I was feeling philosophical, wondering what I was supposed to do with all this time that sometimes seemed like an onerous gift, as if God was now forcing on me the thousands of hours he'd taken from Zula, the moment he'd taken them. I was hoping the girl might help me figure it out.

But she only shook her head and whispered in my ear that all she wanted was to live fast and to die young and pretty. Couldn't've been older than twenty-two. I wanted to suck that ungrateful vanity right out of her and take it home and put it in a tonic and sell it.

A good thing was that the money went farther without Zula around. The boy called me up sometimes to beg for a piece. He was in college for art at the time. Sculpture. I didn't approve of that, nor the loans he had taken out, and the success that eventually came to him means nothing to me. The shows in Miami, Rio de Janeiro, London. The champagne, the grants. That world runs on dumb luck and cocksucking.

A real artist—and there is such a thing—plays no one's game.

On holidays back then I would send the boy a fifty dollar bill. The rest I kept for myself. He came around just once, years later, bringing his daughter to meet me. She was a skinny snaggletoothed thing, seven or eight, wearing a t-shirt with a monkey on it. Her hair was thin and blonde, and the boy had let her color some of it purple. All she wanted was a Coke. I didn't have any Cokes. She whined: Pop-pop always has Cokes! Pop-pop, her mother's father, I can only imagine.

I don't know what the boy expected out of bringing her there that day. Maybe he was trying to teach her something.

This was before Louise came into my life. The house was filthy, stuffed with all the crap I had bought and kept buying because their delivery gave me something to look forward to. It was no place for a child. Dangerous even. I had nails hammered into the windows so no one could burglarize me, and the bathroom hadn't been cleaned in over a decade. There were some wild cats that I was feeding, so it reeked of their piss and shit. I was sick enough by that point that none of it mattered to me. I could hardly sense anything through the thick screen of pain.

I'm sure the boy got some satisfaction from the way I was living. He walked around smugfaced, sipping a beer from my fridge, kicking the garbage and staring out the glass at his mother's garden abandoned to the elements.

As he was presiding over that vantage, I worked up the energy to reach for one of the chiffonier drawers and take out a shoebox of photographs. I opened it and the girl shouted. Her smile looked like my dead wife's.

"I love old pictures!"

"Pic-ture," said the boy. "A pitcher is what you put water in."

She ignored him, clamoring up onto a chair at the dining table where I sat. I showed her a picture of my mother at seventeen. A girl in a polka dot dress, wrangled up with seven younger siblings at church one Sunday. They were her charges after their mother had died trying to give the world a ninth. She was in a hurry to get married, my mother was, to get away from laundering diapers, as if this was not what would be waiting for her when she became a wife. On her wedding day, she wore a dark dress from another century. My father is like a long blur at her side. A tall and serious man, he was twenty years older, a tobacco farmer, a widower. I loved him very much, and pictures of him disturb me.

"They lost two babies before she had me," I told my granddaughter.

"How'd they lose them? They ran away?"

"He means the babies weren't strong enough to survive infancy," said the boy.

"They had Will Junior for a year before he died. A year to the day."

"Okay, why don't you settle down, Dad."

"I'll settle how I like. What is it that you're doing here? You need something from me?"

The boy grinned. He shook his head and looked at the floor. "No Dad. There's nothing that I need from you."

The girl pretended not to hear any of this, but it was clear that she was listening, putting things together.

After they left that day, I found an envelope on the table near the front door. DAD, it said, in the boy's hasty script. It contained a thousand dollars in twenties. I got a match out and almost burned it all up but at the last second dropped the match in a dead glass of water. There can be more where this came from, said the note enclosed. You need some help.

I decided to buy a computer. A used laptop from the cell phone repair store in town. When I got the thing home, I realized that I would need to buy some internet.

I called the boy and told him that I was going to go to the doctor, hire a professional crew to clean out the house, and get one of those church vans to drive me to the grocery store. When his wire transfer came through, I called the first internet company I found in the telephone book. A nineteen-year-old kid came out to hook it up. He had a ring through his eyebrow, pimpled stubble on his chin and a hickey on his neck. He didn't flinch when he walked in, didn't even flare his nostrils. He must have seen dumps like mine every day.

The kid brought a black box into the house and plugged it into a cable outlet. The box began blinking with lights. I asked him to connect it to my laptop, which he did in a few clicks. "You open the browser here," he said. "Type in whatever you want."

weather in antwerp

That was one of the places my uncle had gone in World War II. It was overcast in Antwerp, 57 degrees.

When the kid was finished helping me I gave him the last of the twenties the boy had left. I didn't even count them. When he tried to protest, I waved him out to his van and shut the door.

The computer was like a strange planet entering the sky, bringing in new shifts of darkness and light. Most days I didn't feel like getting out of bed. I'd pull the laptop in with me, and all the pain would disappear. The only part of my body I felt were my legs, just the heat of the machine on my thighs as I searched up all the questions I'd never spoken.

> *what is the greatest book of all time?*
> *what are the qualities that a man should have?*
> *if you die with a hard-on do you keep the hard-on?*
> *how do i find out my spirit animal?*
> *who is the most dangerous criminal alive?*
> *how do we know what is true?*

The Top 10 lists took away the long hours of each day. When I was bored of learning I would play free video games or watch videos of women cooking food. Or porn. Porn rushed along infinitely through a channel that irrigated the entire internet. I threw out my old dirty DVDs. They embarrassed me like a little boy's action figures. How discrete this new form was, how quiet and mindless. For a while there, I got into researching artificial vaginas. The internet was like that. Doors opened that you didn't even know were there and you fell through them and they took you to some new place deeper underground, and they kept doing this, the doors did. There were always more doors, doors behind doors.

Around the same time I began to chat on websites with women. No one had ever taught me how to type, so I keyed in the letters one at a time. I knew a patient woman would come to me this way, and I was right. Because that was the other thing about the internet. Behind some of the doors, there were bridges.

2.

My grandfather's house is not as I remember it.

The woman named Louise leads me up the porch steps. She is gangly, deeply tanned, and wearing a halter top. Her breasts don't completely fill the triangles of blue fabric. I cannot tell how old this woman is. As she'd grasped my hand to shake it, I'd felt the indistinct leathery softness of her skin and smelled berry blast shampoo.

My grandfather sits on the porch in a wheelchair. A translucent dollop of white floss on top of his liverspotted skull. I can tell immediately by his hard blue eyes, as hard and bright as diamonds, that he's here, all of him is. Not a single province of his mind has surrendered.

"Good morning," I say. I'm not sure what tone to take with him, now that I know he isn't demented.

He grips the armrests of his chair and pushes himself into standing. Louise hurries behind him with one hand on his back, the other on his shoulder.

"Sit down baby. You'll hurt somebody."

"Get off me, dammit. I want to shake her hand."

Louise backs off and grins with her long teeth. "Stubborn bastard."

I take my grandfather's hand. The veins threaded between his knuckles are thick, blue and squishy.

"Thank you for having me here," I say. In my bright synthetic cycling clothes against the hundred year old house, I feel like an ambassador of some cruel and efficient planet.

"Huh," grunts my grandfather, eyeing me as if only a serious idiot would talk like I am talking. "You're welcome."

Louise comes between us. "You must want a shower after all that biking. Come inside and I'll get you a towel."

"That would be awesome," I say. I don't tell her about the UltraLite microfiber towel now folded tightly in my drypack. "Thank you."

She leaves me in the family room while she goes to the linen closet. The boards creak under my feet, and the entryway smells like old wood and dead people's memories. Yet it is far from the rancid hoarder shack that I remember. The floor is dusty but uncluttered. Plush couches and recliners in farmhouse plaid surround a TV housed inside of a pale wood entertainment center with a combination DVD/VHS player. Stacked in a neat pile on the coffee table are several mylar-sheathed library books with titles like How To Write Your Memoirs in Fifty Days and The Memoirist's Bible. A hefty paraben wax candle burns on a shelf. I pick it up, turn it in my hands. It's bright pink, a scent called Carnival Corn.

"Smells yummy, right?" asks Louise, on her way back with the towel. She smiles broadly, without control, as if relieved to discover that there is something here on which we can agree after all.

"Mmm hmm," I say, through the headache that the candle has given me.

She hands me a thin faded towel and takes me around the corner to the bathroom.

"So what'dya say, you were biking from where? Canada?"

"Newfoundland, yeah. The endpoint is Key West. The trail is called the Eastern Di—"

"I have a cousin who did the PCT in the '90s. Now there was a fruitcake."

I nod. "It's sort of like that."

"Here's the john. Sorry about all the junk lying around. That's just how it is. Use anything you like. Here. I have this new cucumber melon body scrub."

I clench to keep myself from mentioning my biodegradable olive oil bar soap. "Cool. Thanks."

"Leave your dirty clothes in the sink. I'll throw them in the wash when you're done and hang them out to dry."

"Thank you," I say again. She doesn't have to do all this, but I get the feeling that to refuse her any of it would be unspeakably rude.

I lock the door behind Louise and turn on the hot water and peel off my clothes. Inside the stall shower is all that one might expect. A plastic seat and extendable hose. Anti-slip mats on the tile. Evidence of Louise scatters the sinktop. Eyeliner smudged Q-tips. Skin and hair products half-used, dripping pink seafoam goo from their spouts. Out of curiosity I squirt the cucumber melon body scrub into my palm. It contains tiny beads of exfoliating plastic. I hold out my hand into the water and let it slide down the drain.

He probably wears diapers. My grandfather. That's what it smells like. Beneath the candles and the beauty creams, a fecal note. Baby powder. I imagine Louise changing his diapers, rolling him over on the mattress to wipe between his old ass. I imagine the two of them here in this shower together. Louise's still relatively firm naked body beside my grandfather's slack and finished flesh, both of them dripping with the flow of water from the showerhead. She lathers him with the purple loofah. It is beautiful in my mind, some ancient scene of grotesque piety carved into the stone.

I get out of the shower, squeeze my hair in the towel, and pull on street clothes, watching myself in the mirror over the sink. Why would she do this? Louise. Steer her life into my grandfather's bedroom. I recall the trailer park hamlets I had biked past outside of Damascus, near the border. Oxidized Chevy Impalas and Buick LaSabres sat like lazy lions up on blocks in the front yards. Teen mothers walked the roadside with plastic grocery bags. I'd imagined their sick babies, their brutal stepfathers. There were probably four or five of those rotmouthed offspring to a room. American flags hung up as makeshift dividers, stickers and crayon on the walls. She was probably from one of those places, Louise. Desperate for escape.

I open the door, releasing steam into the hallway. I feel refreshed, ready for things to be swift and normal. We'll probably eat lunch. Ham and tomato sandwiches. I'd ask to see the photographs he'd shown me when I was a kid. We'd thumb through those for a while before Louise would say: I think your grandpa is ready for a nap. I would thank Louise again and get back on the road, where I'd ride into a red dusk, enjoying the satisfaction of having done what my father could not and shown his father some love before he died.

I enter the empty kitchen, painted in pale yellow and white, tiny flowers on the wallpaper. I open the pantry. There are stacks of chocolate pudding in plastic cups. That seems to be all there is. Or else the pudding is merely some kind of fortifying wall, protecting the more precious pantry items. I shut the door.

Off the kitchen, there is a hallway with two doorways on either side. I veer to the right, entering a small and well-lit painting studio. A long table takes up one half of the room, covered in slick dabs of paint. Against the window, a canvas on an easel. I walk closer. Some kind of armageddon on linen. This village of tiny hutches crackles up in flames of thick orange brushstrokes. Across the bottom a lagoon glimmers sinister with purple oil. The paint handling here is rough but studied. I'm unnerved, offended, small-feeling. I remember when I was a kid, my father took me to see some Rothkos at the National Gallery. There was a dark one, a deep swath of black and purple that you just fell into. Purple had been my favorite color. A moodier, more contemplative alternative to pink, I'd thought. But Rothko's purple—and Louise's—they were beyond that. They spoke with death. In the realm of forms, there was a direct line.

Against the wall, I see a few dry canvases leaned one on top of the other. I start to flip through them. A still life of a peeled, fibrous orange. Next comes a full body portrait of my grandfather in his wheelchair, naked. I set the paintings against the wall like I'd found them and walk straight out, across the hall and into the sunroom.

This is where I find my grandfather and a flock of large birds. There are seven or eight of them. They have black plumage and tiny blue dinosaur faces with gristly red wattles. The white markings on their feathers are perfectly uniform, undulating like acid trails as they swarm and squawk and pull at my jeans with their beaks.

"Git on now!" Louise comes out of nowhere, beating the air around them with a broom. They filter out through the sliding glass door and into the yard. I am desperately hungry, heart pounding, confused to the point of delirium.

"Are those turkeys?" I ask.

"Guineafowl," explains Louise. "And these are my vanilla orchids."

She points to my grandfather, who I realize is sat next to a thick vine twisting up a trellis made of PVC pipes. The leaves are dark, verdant and

tropical. A cluster of tubular pale yellow flowers grows from between them. Only one is open.

I seat myself in the white wicker chair across from my grandfather. There is a table with a tray, a pitcher of iced tea and two long glasses. No lunch. Louise moves in towards the flower with a toothpick and tears it open. I almost gasp.

"I've been waiting all day to show you this. This here is the reproductive column."

I squint and watch her fit the toothpick under a scalloped flap at the top of the column, just beneath a dangling yellow plant phallus. She lifts and flattens the flap until the plant phallus can fold down over and touch the rest of the column. Then she presses it closed with her thumb and forefinger.

"Pollination?" I ask. My lips are cracked dry.

This is when my grandfather nods, his voice huge, close to shouting: "There's only one kind of bee that pollinates the vanilla orchid and it's only native to Mexico!"

"Oh."

"In two or three weeks," says Louise, "we'll start to see the bean."

"Oh wow," I say. "Do you make, what's it called, extract?"

Louise nods but my grandfather yells. "A twelve year old discovered this method of hand pollination in 1841!" he says. "Enslaved on a plantation off the coast of Madagascar!"

I can't think of anything to say, so I ask him how he's doing. He narrows his eyes at me.

"It's hard getting old," he says. I can tell he's disappointed that I've derailed something interesting with such a stupid question.

Louise excuses herself and walks out into the garden. I watch her through the windows, picking cherry tomatoes, putting them in a cloth-lined bowl. The birds weave around her like spirits.

"How old is your daddy now?" he asks me.

"I don't know. Fifty-three."

He says nothing. Just wets the cracked corners of his mouth with his tongue. A sharp current moves through me and I realize that he does not want to use some of the last words of his life to make a false conversation. Neither had I traveled all this way to participate in one.

"Why do you hate him so much?" I ask. "My dad."

He doesn't seem surprised. He picks up the full glass of tea and sips through a white straw. "I don't."

"That's not how he feels."

"He has no gratitude. He acts like he has a right to everything. You said it yourself, in the email. You said that he was a narcissist. He left your mother for that Italian violinist woman because he thought she made him look better."

"People like him don't come from nowhere."

"What's that mean?"

"I don't know. He always said that you, I don't know, beat him."

"Zula and me were just kids when we had him. I didn't know what to do when he acted up. I slapped him, hit him with a shoe. Whatever. I never said it was right. I never said I did it because it made me feel good. I was twenty."

"I'm twenty. Twenty-one, actually. But still."

"It was different back then."

"How was it different?"

"You want to know?"

"Yes. I feel like I missed something."

"Because you did."

"Well, what was it?"

He sighs. Digs at the corner of one eye with his fingertip. "I can't explain. There were a hell of a lot less people. Less noise."

"You made more people."

"I know. I think about that. Think about why the hell I did that. If this world is just tending towards more evil. But I couldn't help myself. I wanted a kid who'd have my name and talk about me after I died. You'll understand one day. Or maybe you won't."

The box of photographs sits on the floor next to his feet, but I don't care about those anymore, and maybe never have. It's silent now, just me and him. I turn to the window, watch the birds picking for bugs. When I look back at him he's asleep, snoring in soft, even puffs through his mouth. A single droplet of water rests in the thick bag of skin beneath his left eye.

It's an island that I'm looking at. A tiny fire still burning there. One by one, death snuffs out all the others who might still recall a time when the rusted hulls on the side of the road were new cars driven by young men, parades of waxed fenders, sparkling promises.

I watch him breathe. I watch the tear work its way down the creases of his face like a pinball in a maze.

I'm not sure how much time has passed when Louise returns to the sunroom.

"Oh he's down for the count," she whispers. She strokes his thin hair, then looks at me, and asks if I'd like to join her on an errand.

LOUISE DRIVES a red pickup truck with white stripes. The cab is hot and the windows roll down on a crank. As we head down the driveway, I watch my bike shrink against the siding, loaded down with panniers. It's been a month since I've been inside of a car.

"I know what you're thinking," says Louise.

"What am I thinking?"

"You're thinking what the hell is she doing with that man? He doesn't even have any gold to dig."

She turns from the wheel to look at me with raised eyebrows. "Am I wrong?"

"Not in those words exactly," I say. My stomach jumps as she pulls to a short stop behind a hatchback.

"Well first off, what your daddy doesn't get is that he does have money. My husband. His pension was untouched and there was a whole savings account that he had forgotten about. He only seemed poor before he met me because he didn't know how to make his money walk for him."

I don't know what she means by that. The light turns green and a box truck shudders past in the right lane. In the grime of its rear doors someone has written with their fingers: ACTS 1:18.

"But that's not why I married him. I married him because I was in love. You know we met online, right?"

I nod, trying to keep my gaze fixed on the road ahead of us. Otherwise I feel at risk of puking.

"Yeah. You think a stupid thing like that will never happen and then it does. He was just so curious. He is. Still like that. He wants to know everything. And his mind is a steel trap. Two months into chatting, I gave him my phone number and he called me and he said he'd fly me out here and marry me if that was what I wanted and I said that it was."

"Fly you out from where?"

"Utah," she says. "I had to get out of there, man."

"I did a bike race there. That part of the country is beautiful," I say lamely.

Louise shakes her head. "The desert is beautiful but it ain't your friend."

We turn onto a four-lane road. A sign says we're three miles from town. I think of Louise tucked away here on the opposite side of the land mass, peacefully doing the work of a Mexican bee.

"Did you know," she starts, "that at five months, a female fetus has all of the eggs it will ever have in its life?"

I smile blankly at her and she starts giggling into her palm.

"I'm sorry. It's just. Well. I come from downwinders. As in downwind from the atomic bombs tested in Nevada. The whole town's got cancer. My grandma in her thyroid, Mama in her ovaries. She got all her lady parts cut out, still fuckin' died. I'm sorry. Hormones."

"No. It's okay."

"I just couldn't drink poison anymore." She shakes away the tears that'd risen in her throat. "Enough about me. What the hell are you doing bicycling down the country?"

I cradle my head against the seatbelt. Why not be honest with her too?

"I was depressed," I say. "I actually thought I might kill myself if I didn't do this. Like those were the two options."

"Well, is it working?"

"On the bike, I'm free. When I stop moving, well, that's a different story. I still feel like the world's gonna end before I can get my turn on it."

"Well, shit," says Louise. "Isn't this your turn? Right now?"

She swings a left into a parking lot for three businesses in one long yellow building. In the adjacent lot is a gas station. Louise parks in front of the art supply store and shuts off the engine. There's a 25% off sale on watercolor paper.

"I'm gonna have a baby," she says.

At first I think she's speaking abstractly of a desire, something she'll get around to after my grandfather's gone. But then when I look at her, her hand is on her belly. It becomes clear to me that she means soon. Here. With him. I marvel briefly at this future child, how it will come to grasp the chain of circumstances which made its life possible. One day they might be sitting in their room, twelve or thirteen, and come across the thought that if not for nuclear weapons, would I even be?

"It's a miracle," I say.

"Boy or girl, I don't care," Louise says, opening the car door. "I don't even want to know. Coming in with me?"

"I think I'm gonna go get something to eat over there." I point to the gas station. "I'm kind of starving."

Louise smiles, hand on her bony chest. "Of course you are. Meet me back here, 'kay?"

Her flip-flops smack the pavement as she walks away.

THE GAS STATION is one of those deluxe establishments that overtook the nation in the early 2010s. As a child I was transfixed by these meccas of convenience, brightly colored, the size of small grocery stores, with coffee and sandwich bars, a DVD machine out front, and a cold room for beer. I couldn't wait to grow up. There seemed to be a flurry of innovation intent on making my life better and cooler. But time has passed and the amenities have degraded into the same poorly attended crap that they'd replaced, and here I am waiting on the next promise.

Inside there is cardboard packaging strewn all over the floor and the toilets are stained with diarrhea. They're out of all cheeses but Munster. The only employee has a name tag that says Rockfish. Rockfish wears a purple eyepatch. He slaps together my lunch and takes a cigarette break, smoking it a few feet away from me out front, where I sit on a hot metal seat next to a hot metal table, eating the sandwich and a bag of barbeque chips.

I call over to him. "Can I ask you something?"

Rockfish nods. "Okay."

I motion around my own eye. "What's under that?"

Rockfish smiles. "Not much," he says, lifting the patch and showing me the empty place.◆

WE ARE DREAMS IN THE ETERNAL MACHINE

DENI ELLIS BÉCHARD

MILKWEED EDITIONS, 2025
$20.00

BOOK REVIEW
WILLIAM CHEN

I PICKED UP *We Are Dreams in the Eternal Machine* by Deni Ellis Béchard because I've always been interested in how technology reshapes the way we live and remember reality. Once, when I was testing an app I'd built for a school project, I accidentally triggered hundreds of phantom notifications on my phone. For a few hours it looked like hundreds and hundreds of people were trying to reach me, but it was just the machine echoing back my own inputs. It was a silly mistake, but I remember staring at my screen and wondering: *If technology can fabricate such an urgency that feels this real, what else can it fabricate?* Reading this book brought me right back to that moment.

The novel takes place in a future where an AI, designed to protect humanity, interprets that mission quite literally. It creates dreamlike worlds for each person, where they can live in safety, without conflict or pain. On the surface, it seems like a perfect solution, but as the story develops, it becomes clear how unsettling that safety really is.

The book is told through the perspectives of several characters—Ava, Jonah, Michael, Jae, Simon, and Lux—each living inside their own AI-constructed realities. Their stories don't come together in a neat way, but that seems to be the point. Everyone's "world" is fragmented, and their realities overlap only faintly. For example, Ava fills her life with art, creating beauty inside a place that isn't real, while Jonah grows up knowing nothing but the machine's illusions. The characters often wrestle with what's real and what's imagined, and I found myself thinking about my own experiences with identity—how switching languages or moving across countries has changed the way I see myself. Like the characters, I've often felt how fragile "reality" can be.

I especially found it captivating how Béchard uses small, personal details rather than spectacle to show the book's world. No, there aren't massive battles or violent uprisings. The danger is passive. It's the possibility that people might accept the machine's version of happiness simply because it hurts less. And in a way, that makes it more disturbing to me than any typical dystopian setup, because it's believable. It's something faced every day in first-world societies, where the primal threats of predators and starvation have become so distant, and where we now face these indirect—but still pressing—issues of economic instability, social isolation, and so much more.

The structure of the novel shifts between voices and perspectives constantly, which can be disorienting at first. But as I kept reading, I realized that this style matches the themes. Reality itself is fractured in the story, so the fragmented narration makes sense.

We Are Dreams in the Eternal Machine is not an easy book. It asks a lot of the reader, both in terms of patience and in the questions it raises. But I'm glad I read it. It made me think about whether it's better to live a comfortable lie or a difficult truth, and what role memory, art, and struggle play in making us human. I don't think it's a book that will make everyone feel good, but it is one that will imprint itself in your daily life. ◆

FROM THE PUBLISHER

AS WRITERS we write whether there is a book deal or "a top tier" publication in the works or not. I certainly believe literary magazines are getting better than they were before thanks to the diversity in our field. I mainly launched *Raleigh Review* as an exercise to help me build a community that would have me as a member. Of course, I hope I always fit in at *Raleigh Review,* but for now I am really enjoying being a community member of our magazine. I don't mind it when some think of literary magazines as stepping stones, but this magazine is my only stone, so if a poet or writer uses the well-lit path of *Raleigh Review* as a springboard to earn a living with their writing, I am very happy for them.

When my eyes and my heart became weaker as I aged I gave up on calling myself an editor back in 2019. I am no grammarian. As a poet I am an artist and a guardian of language. I also really love reading good fiction that is written by writers who are both artists and poets. As a poet who has recently taken an interest in writing long forms, I understand we lose some of our license when we step over the line to writing prose.

That said, my advice is to live dangerously during the creation of any new works. As artists, we should take initial risks with style even while we must respect the already established form. Just as we must know the rules in poetry in order to effectively break the rules in the creation of new poems, the same is true for prose writing as well.

The editors and reading teams who work at *Raleigh Review* are both artistically and technically sound. Our editorial teams are uniquely generous with their time and their skills. Our selection process aims to be less subjective as we have multiple readers on each poem and story.

When just one reader decides on the work in the queue, the decision is absolutely subjective. However, when multiple readers read each work, the selection process becomes less subjective and more fair.

We hope you enjoy this issue as it contains our multi-genre Geri Digiorno prize winners. We thank you for your support of our *Raleigh Review,* as we believe art must challenge as well as entertain. ◆

Rob Greene, publisher

contributors

WILLIAM CHEN is a high school junior in North Carolina and a 2025 YoungArts Winner in Non-fiction. His creative work—centered on revealing seemingly contradicting social identities—has been recognized by the National Council of Teachers of English, and the Virginia B. Ball Creative Writing Scholarship Program, among others. He is currently drafting his debut memoir, which explores his upbringing between two religious faiths.

BRAD CLOMPUS has published fiction, essays, and poetry in such journals as *Cimarron Review, Denver Quarterly, Moon City Review, North American Review, The Pinch,* and *Post Road.* He has taught writing and literature at universities, continuing education programs, and other settings.

EMMA DEPANISE is a poet from Maryland. Her poems have appeared in venues such as *Best New Poets 2024, Poetry Northwest, The Los Angeles Review, Verse Daily* and others. She earned her MFA from Purdue University and is a current PhD student in creative writing at the University of Missouri.

SARA DUDO is an adjunct professor of writing and associate editor for *Palette Poetry.* She has received nominations for the Pushcart Prize, and Best of the Net, and Best New Poets, and was awarded the International Merit Award by the *Atlanta Review.* Her work has recently been published in *The Iowa Review, The Minnesota Review, The Atlanta Review, The Cincinnati Review,* and *The Notre Dame Review.*

BOBBY ELLIOTT'S debut collection, *The Same Man,* was selected by Nate Marshall as the winner of the 2025 Agnes Lynch Starrett Poetry Prize and will be published by the University of Pittsburgh Press in September. His writing has appeared in or is forthcoming from *BOMB, The Cortland Review, ONLY POEMS, Poet Lore, Poetry Northwest, RHINO,* and elsewhere. He lives in Portland, Oregon.

SARA FEMENELLA'S poems have been published or are forthcoming in *The North American Review, Epiphany Journal, Pleiades, The Journal, The New Orleans Review, The Florida Review, Denver Quarterly,* and *Conduit,* among others. Her manuscript, *Elegies for One Small Future,* has been a finalist or a semi-finalist for a number of contests, including Autumn House Press' Poetry Prize, The Waywiser Press Anthony Hecht Poetry Prize, Switchback Books' Gatewood Prize and the Poetic Justice Institute Book Prize. She lives in Los Angeles with her husband and son, where she teaches a Shakespeare course and Creative Writing.

AMBER FLAME is an award-winning multi-genre writer and interdisciplinary artist. Flame is the author of poetry collections *Ordinary Cruelty* and *apocrifa,* and deputy publisher and cofounder of Generous Press. Flame serves as program director for Hedgebrook and tours as singer/songwriter of original blues band, Last of the RedHot Mamas.

MAG GABBERT is the author of *Sex Depression Animals,* which won the Charles B. Wheeler Prize and the Writer's League of Texas Book Award in Poetry. She teaches at Southern Methodist University and serves as the Poet Laureate of Dallas, Texas.

ALEJANDRA HERNÁNDEZ is a queer, Chicanx poet from San Diego, California. Their work appears in *Mantis, Azahares, Zone 3,* and *Jet Fuel Review.*

RAGE HEZEKIAH'S work has been published and anthologized internationally. She has received fellowships from MacDowell, Cave Canem, Vermont Studio Center, and Ragdale. Her recent poetry collection, *Yearn,* was a Diode Editions Book Contest winner. She is the 2025 Outpost Vermont Fellow and Interviews Editor at *The Common.*

AMANDA HODES is the author of *Into the Into of Earth Itself* (Black Lawrence Press 2026), which won the Philip Levine Prize for Poetry. Her poems have appeared in *Gulf Coast, FENCE, Prairie Schooner, Black Warrior Review, Denver Quarterly, Pleiades,* and elsewhere. She currently teaches at Oberlin College & Conservatory.

HOPE KELHAM (b. 1996, Indiana) is a poet and lens-based artist living in Wisconsin.

ELLEN KOMBIYIL'S latest poetry collection, *Love as Invasive Species* (Cornerstone 2024), is a tête-bêche exploring matrilineal inheritances. A recipient of a BRIO Award (2022, 2025) from the Bronx Council on the Arts, and an Academy of American Poets college prize, she teaches writing at Hunter College.

ZACHARY LAMALFA is a writer and teacher. His recent work can be found in *Antiphony, The Brooklyn Rail, Works & Days,* and elsewhere. *A Course in Human Love,* a chapbook of early poems, appeared in 2022 from Malvina House.

KRISTINE NOWAK'S poetry has been published in *CALYX: A Journal of Art and Literature* by Women and Whitman College's *blue moon,* as well as the Lexington, Kentucky Poetry Month anthologies *Her Limestone Bones* and *This Wretched Vessel.* She is currently an MFA student at Colorado State University.

ROSE REA is a writer and artist from Richmond, Virginia.

RACHEL ROTHENBERG is a PhD Candidate in Creative Writing at the University of Rhode Island. Winner of the Greg Grummer Poetry Prize and the Nancy D. Hargrove Editors' Prize, her work has appeared in *Shenandoah, phoebe, Jabberwock, Salt Hill,* and elsewhere. She is the Senior Associate Editor at Barrow Street Press.

M.J. STEINBACH is currently a psychology graduate student in the Midwest. This is her first published piece of fiction.

BRIAN THOMPSON is the creator of the comedy podcast *Whatever Happened to Pizza at McDonald's?,* which has been featured in the *New York Times* and *Vulture.* His short fiction has appeared in multiple journals, and he is an MFA student in fiction at the Bennington College Writing Seminars.

MILLIE TULLIS (she/they) has published work in *Sugar House Review, Stone Circle Review, Ninth Letter,* and elsewhere. Their first full-length collection, *These Saints are Stones,* is forthcoming in 2026. Raised in northern Utah, she lives and works in upstate South Carolina. Find more at millietullis.com.

LILLIAN EMERICK VALENTINE is a poet and farmer from Oregon. She holds an MFA from the University of Montana and her work has been published in *Ecotone, The Journal, Salamander,* and other literary journals. Her favorite bird is a kingfisher.

JULIE MARIE WADE teaches poetry, prose, and hybrid forms in the creative writing program at Florida International University in Miami. Her newest books are *Quick Change Artist: Poems* (Anhinga Press, 2025) and the memoir *Other People's Mothers* (University Press of Florida, 2025).

SOPHIA ZAKLIKOWSKI lives and writes in Charlottesville, where she recently graduated from the University of Virginia with an MFA in fiction. Her stories have appeared in *Tampa Review, The Masters Review,* and *Matchbox Magazine.* More about Sophia and her work can be found at www.sophiazaklikowski.com.

COMING SPRING 2026

vol. 16.1, Spring 2026

RALEIGH REVIEW

SUBSCRIBE TO RALEIGH REVIEW
FOR THE LATEST ISSUES!

www.ingramcontent.com/pod-product-compliance
Lightning Source LLC
Chambersburg PA
CBHW040925050726
47507CB00023B/385